# *The Secrets of*

"Whatsoever ye shall ask in prayer, believing, ye shall receive" (Matthew 22:23)

'A man who acquires the ability to take full possession of his own mind may take possession of anything else to which he is justly entitled." (Carnegie)

## ASK * BELIEVE * RECEIVE

I dedicate this novel to my friend Christine...thank you for inspiring me and teaching me about the Secret in the first place, and to Ken who opened my mind even further.

I also dedicate this journey into mystery, empathy and true gratitude to my own personal lucky Irish charm Paul and most of all to Nicky and my family who are my world and constant support.

Gabi took the big door key out of her pocket. She had just returned from her daily walk on the beach. The late autumn sun warmed her back; Millie, the border collie that belonged to her son, looked expectantly at her.

"Yes Millie, Nick will soon be home! He can take you out for another walk later!" Every time she approached her beautiful Manor House overlooking the bay of St Ives, she was stunned by its beauty, especially in the sun. She loved the colour play on the stained-glass door. Only 6 months after she first laid eyes on this property she actually held the keys in her hand and once again she said a silent thank you to the universe for having enabled her to make this place her home, hers, Paddy's and Nicks. She still sometimes struggled to believe – after all she did not come from a wealthy background and from the first day of her moving to the UK from her home country Germany she had struggled to make ends meet, even though she had always worked hard to support herself and her son after her divorce. And buying this house had nothing to do with having worked hard in her job.... moving to Cornwall, moving to this house was simply but truly down to magic! Down to the magic within – it was a dream come true. Everything had all of a sudden fallen into place. And now her life was pure joy – no worries at all.

"Martha, we are back!" Gabi wiped the dog's paws and went through the spacious hall to the kitchen.

"Tea and fresh scones are ready!" Martha was indeed a jewel. Gabi had met her in a small café in St Ives. The two women were approximately the same age; Martha was a widow looking for company more than a job. Hence when the two got chatting, Gabi who had just moved to her new home, simply offered her the position as housekeeper. And she soon realised that that might just have been one of the best decisions in her life. Millie was already chewing the treat Martha had given her.

"Are you joining me on the balcony, Martha?" Gabi took the prepared tray and led the way to the balcony with the simply awesome view over the Bay of St Ives. The afternoon sun was certainly warm enough to sit outside and enjoy the fresh brew.

"Yes, I think I will!" Martha smiled. The two women sat down at the table, and Martha poured the first cups. "What a beautiful day this is! More and more often now we get warm autumns after not so ideal summers. The climate has certainly changed."

"Yes, so it has. But as long as we have days like this at any time of the year I certainly won't moan!" Gabi smiled and put some clotted cream and home-made strawberry jam on the fresh scone. "Mhm, Martha this is delightful!"

Martha smiled. "I think Mr Paddy is quite partial to the Cornish scones, too, even though he claims that he does not have a sweet tooth. Almost as partial as to the cooked breakfasts!"

Like everyone else Martha was quite smitten with Paddy, Gabi's partner for close to a year now. Paddy had appeared in Gabi's life out of nowhere. Neither of them had actually been looking for yet another relationship, but they had met and very quickly realised that indeed their paths had crossed for the purpose of bringing them together for each other and the greater good of humanity, as they were both truly empathic souls wanting to pass their understanding of the ways of the universe and their personal experiences on to all those in this world who struggled with their own demons, whatever they were.

"Yes, it amazes me again and again how Paddy retains his athletic figure, considering his love for high calorie breakfasts and indulgent local treats."

"He walks it off. Much like Nick. By the way, I have pre-cooked all Nick's favourite dishes and froze them in portions for him to take back to university on Sunday."

"You really spoil us, Martha!" Gabi put her hand on Martha's arm as a tender gesture of gratitude.

"Nonsense – you three are my family now."

Gabi nodded. Paddy worked in Real Estate and travelled a lot; however, his true calling was counselling therapy. He had an amazing ability at reading people and was more than brilliant at helping them sort their lives. It was the shared interest in the psychology of the human being and in counselling that had first brought Gabi and Paddy together.

"Anything here for me?" Nick had stepped out on the terrace giving both women a kiss on the cheek and then cuddling his dog.

"Plenty." Martha poured him a cuppa and handed him a scone – of course without raisins. "Quite a nice day!" Nick had been out surfing with his local mates and certainly looked the part. Gabi was so proud of her handsome son, now nicely tanned and self-confident. He studied Law in the North, so only came down to Cornwall every few months. Millie rested under the table, her head on Nick's feet.

"Is Paddy going to be back, before I am heading off to Uni?"

Gabi nodded. "I expect him back the latest tomorrow evening."

"Good, because I really hoped to spend some time with him, too." Without any effort on Paddy's side he had quickly won Nick over; they both shared a passion for sports, and Paddy was a great listener who gave advice and support in a very calm and collected way. Nick had come to really enjoy his company after the initial awkwardness of having to get used to a new man in his mother's life.

Just then Gabi's mobile rang. She checked; it was her publisher. "Got to take this, excuse me." She got up, answered and walked through to the library.

"Has mum finished her next novel already?" Nick grabbed another scone.

"Almost. Paddy being away quite a bit recently has given her the time to go through the manuscript again, proof-read and make the changes that she discussed with her friend Chris, when he came over a few weeks ago."

Nick nodded. "Chris is great. What a character!"

"I just love how your mum and Chris support each other in their work. To listen to the two of them, is so rewarding. There is no rivalry at all, considering they are both authors."

"I guess, they understand each other. And they both had to struggle to get where they are today."

"Mhm – there is that. And there is also the understanding of the importance of gratitude in both of them." Martha got up to collect all the china on the big tray, when a loud bang startled them all and made Millie jump.

"What on earth?????" Nick got up and turned to go inside. His mother appeared in the door.

"I am not sure what that was, but it came from under the house."

"Exciting, shall we look for secret passageways!" Nick dashed to his room and came back with a huge torch. His mother smiled at him.

"Great yes, let's see, if we can find a way from up here down to the smuggler's cove. I would actually not be surprised...after all, we are on top of one of the rocks overlooking the bay."

For the next hour they went through the downstairs rooms – the big library, the living room, pantry and kitchen, Gabi's study, Paddy's office. They knocked on the walls for hidden passageways, even tested the floor for possibly overlooked trap doors. Nothing.

"Maybe the old wine cellar?" Martha who had done the washing up and put the dinner on now came to join the other two.

"Gosh, yes – I forgot about that." They went through the pantry into the kitchen garden and then on to a little outhouse which contained a stairway down under the house to an old cellar. Gabi with her still existing arachnophobia usually avoided the cellar, but of course it was used for storing wine, root vegetables and hardy fruit as well as some jars of chutneys and jams. Nick led the way with his torch until Martha pointed out the light switch.

Having climbed down about ten steps they looked at the solid rock walls around. Using a stick and knocking at the wall, they tried to listen for hollow sounds. Nothing. Then all of a sudden, another loud bang. Gabi's hand on the rock could actually feel a vibration.

"Well it is definitely connected to our rock. I think going to the pub and talking to the locals might help. Might have to schedule this in for the Saturday evening or so." Gabi felt a certain excitement. She of course loved all the smuggler and pirate stories along this coast.

Millie who had not come down those suspicious looking steps with them started her excitement bark.

"A visitor?" Martha turned around and led the way back upstairs.

As they stepped out into the sunlight before even seeing him, Gabi knew it was Paddy. Her heart lifted. He had been gone 10 days.

"Millie, calm down now, you crazy dog. Where is everyone?"

"Here Mr Paddy, exploring the secrets of the house." Martha gave him a quick hug and disappeared into the kitchen.

Millie left Paddy and jumped at Nick who was her clear favourite. "Good to see you back!" He shook hands with Paddy and then threw a stick for Millie.

Finally, it was Gabi's turn to welcome her man. She just smiled at him. His eyes found hers, and they both knew what words could not express anyhow. He opened his arms, and Gabi followed the invite. "I really have missed you, Paddy!" she whispered in his ear. "Gabi, it is good to be home." He kissed her on the forehead, her nose and then on her lips.

He was singing. Gabi smiled at him. He looked at her with a cheeky twinkle in his eyes. He considered himself a naturally good singer, after all...he was Irish. They had both been through a fair share of relationships that went wrong or simply did not work out...a way for the human soul to grow.

Now though they were together; their grown-up children came to see them as much as they could. They all loved being with Gabi and Paddy, one of the reasons was without doubt the tangible harmony in this house. Both Gabi and Paddy had learned their lessons and never shied away from developing further; and now they appreciated life, enjoyed each other and were grateful. In moments like this Gabi reflected on what had brought them together; neither of them was perfect, but they loved each other's imperfections and simply were a perfect match. Looking at him all she could feel was utter love. He continued to sing, lit the candles and poured a drink for both. Paddy had done this house up, it was perfect, and he knew it. He had always had this keen interest in changing objects to make them better. He had a good eye for worthwhile things, for beauty, for giving items a new sparkle just by adding a tiny something or taking away a certain sharpness. He called himself a simple man – yet he expressed himself clearer and better than those Gabi had met who liked to show off their good education.

"How do you like this one?" Paddy loved experimenting with all kind of fruit, herbal extracts, vegetables, juices, mineral water and tonic to create what he called mocktails – non-alcoholic beverages to still excite their taste buds. He was an alcoholic, dry for more than a decade now. He had poured her a glass. Martha stood in the door watching them with a grin.

Gabi took a sip and pulled a face. "I love you to bits, Paddy, but this is a bit on the weird side...a bit too bitter, and too much...is it tarragon, I can taste, in it."

"Point taken and...agreed!" He put his own glass down. "Glass of bubbly for the ladies instead then and some fresh lemon water for me."

Anticipating this rejection, Martha picked the tray up already set and put the bottle and carafe down on the glass table facing the bay window. Paddy sat down next to Gabi, his arm around her, stroking her neck. Then he told the ladies about his recent work trips. Gabi loved listening to him; his Irish accent was so warm and seductive, so full of softness, vibrant tunes; it was also so honest, full of twinkling little fairies and emerald green pastures.

Soon Nick joined them, they had dinner, chats and finally retired. Paddy held Gabi in his arms for a long while after making love. It was this tenderness that gave Gabi all the security and safety she craved. They both slept well. When Gabi woke up in the early hours, she quietly slipped out of bed, put on a dressing gown and sat in the bay window looking out into the sunrise.

She started thinking about how it all had come to be and felt an enormous wave of gratitude inside radiating towards the universe. They say: dreams can come true. They say: never give up. Turning her life around had not been easy; it took willpower, strength, persistence, perseverance and being prepared to face the ridicule of even some of your closest friends, when starting to openly live by the Secret and following the pull of the Law of Attraction. Some people had called her naïve, when she told them that "you are what you think about most of the time"; most people still tell you that you need luck and have to work really hard to get somewhere.

Well, no actually. The truth is that you and you alone are the director of the movie that is your life; your thoughts, your actions will define the path you will walk. By focussing on your beliefs and learning to actually trust your gut feelings and instincts more and more things will fall into place. You will meet the right people for the right reasons at the right time, because you have opened yourself up to the universe. Your vibrations will act as magnets to the people you need to fulfil your dream; without doubt your ultimate goal will be reached. Of course, this does not happen overnight, and neither is it easy. But then again what really matters is that every day you grow, you learn, you develop, and you move another step closer, because you start thinking and feeling the right things.

Gabi smiled into the beautiful colour play of the sunrise over this part of the Cornish coast It had taken her years to reach the point where she could now gratefully say: all is well, I have arrived. But the journey alone with all its learning curves, temporary setbacks and reoccurring doubts had been well worth the effort; not only had it helped her to develop a stronger understanding and deeper empathy, but she had met some amazing people on the way who all played a part in her transformation, either by enriching her life as close friends and / or lovers, by teaching her a lesson, opening her mind to so far completely unknown wisdom, by giving her great memories and heartfelt laughs, beautiful thoughts and eventually by being the person who simply took her hand and walked with her....not ahead not behind, but properly right there beside her. Throughout her life Gabi had met lads and men who she fancied, who fancied her, who she fell in love with, shared her life with for a while or remained forever fascinated by...but nothing compared to this ultimate bliss when totally unexpected, without either of you looking for it you met the one who you instantly know would be your companion going forward. And funnily enough they were not young and beautiful anymore, they both had some major scars inside and out...maybe it was the imperfections that had made them humble enough to accept each other's flaws, give each other the space needed to get ready for honest commitment again and then take the plunge together. In her case it was Paddy – from the very first moment he had got in her car and smiled at her, Gabi had known that the universe had put him in her path to complete her life. It really was the most uplifting feeling, when you for the first time really got the glimpse of an understanding for what it truly meant to bestow your love on another human being that was not your child, parent or sibling...and when the mere thought of this person filled your entire being with peace, calmness, true joy and an utterly amazing influx of positiv energy and constant excitement; and when you could say that your soul had truly found not just another kindred spirit, a soulmate, a sincere friend and tender lover, but when the words of Carl Jung "The meeting of two personalities is like the contact of two chemical substances: if there is any reaction, both are transformed." became innately true, because you could literally feel the energy flow and see it with your inner eye; it was then you realised that life would never be the same again and the deepest, most honest gratitude started flooding your body, so that the only option for you was to walk around with the biggest smile ever all the time. He had been the missing link to materialise...Gabi had still been working in her day job, but had already self-published her first two novels. Bringing their two networks together and Paddy having her back, she finally was put in front of the actual CEO of an important publishing house at the same time as she received an offer for the film rights to her first novel. And from there it had all happened in a whirlwind. She now spent her time writing, mentoring young people in the area and travelling the world speaking and coaching.

Gabi silently left the bedroom and walked to the kitchen. The house was still quiet, even Martha had not got up to prepare some delicacies for breakfast. She got two mugs out and put the kettle on. With two milky coffees, she returned to the bedroom. Paddy had woken up and turned the radio on. She put his mug on his bedside table and returned to her seat in the window. Paddy sat up in bed, arranged the cushions in his back, gave her a big smile, took his mug and closed his eyes again, soaking in the music from their favourite radio station.

Gabi looked at him. She really could not imagine life without him anymore; he was so honest as a human being, so upfront about his demons, full of empathy for others and with a genuine desire to reach out and help, wherever he saw someone struggle. Of course, he was no saint, no one was, but he was a truly good man – someone her dad would have really taken to.

Paddy's lips pulled apart into a big grin. With his eyes still closed, he knew that Gabi had been watching him. "Can you not let your eyes feast on the beauty outside? Or on the content in the book next to you?" It was Gabi's turn to smile. "I love looking at you and reminding myself how blessed I am."

"Wet flannel talk!" He put his mug down and looked at Gabi with his sea blue eyes. They spoke of love, contentment, but also passion and desire. He lifted the blanket and nodded at Gabi. She followed his invitation and snuggled up to him. He embraced her and kissed her forehead, her nose, neck and then the half open lips, as was his little ritual. "Is brea liom tu," he whispered, and she melted.

After breakfast Nick and Paddy took Millie for a walk, while Gabi finished her final editing and then went outside with a fresh cup of tea and her Filofax to check on her next speaking and coaching trips. With her main focus on writing and mentoring, she so far tried to keep her travels to roughly 6 main trips per year. She loved speaking and coaching, but she also loved being home and writing, overlooking the sea, spending time with Martha and her local youth group. Every now and again she managed to coincide her trips with Paddy's; they both enjoyed that, but they also were wise enough to continue to give each other enough space for personal time as well as business. Gabi now had a small office set up in London to look after the back end of her business. Because she had hand picked the right team, she did not really have to be there; her office manager Viv had her full trust and was a simply great organiser. After flicking through her Filofax, she grabbed the phone.

"Hi Viv, its Gabi. Everything ok?" Relaxed she listened to Viv updating her on the sales of her coaching programme, the sales of her books, the news from within the team etc.

"Thank you so much, Viv. I now need you to confirm my travel schedule for the rest of the year. My notebook tells me that I shall be in Germany for a week at the end of September. Then back home. End of October Scotland, early November Scandinavia. Then of course L.A. end of November to see JT and also meet up with the producers of the "Deck of Cards" movie. And that is it, yes?!"

"Yes, that is exactly what I have down in your calendar, Gabi. All the flights are booked and confirmed, as well as the accommodations. Paddy will be in Scotland and Germany with you. He was not sure about L.A., when we last talked. Has he made a decision yet?"

"He only got back last night from his last trip, so I will talk to him later and then let you know. Regarding Christmas…"

"…yes I have already arranged all transfers for your mother and sister and family for being with you from December 23rd at St Ives."

"You are a star, thank you so much, Viv. Can you arrange to accompany me to Scandinavia?"

"If you need me there, of course."

"Great, ok then, you have a good day and I will catch up with you later."

Gabi put all her business stuff back on her desk, grabbed a little handbag with essentials, said bye to Martha and set off down to the harbour. She was just in time to meet Paddy outside the youth club, where she counselled some troubled teenagers, while Paddy talked to the young people struggling already with alcohol and drugs and actually offered counselling therapy.

"Perfect timing, love!" Paddy kissed Gabi and then took her hand. They entered the club house together. Only four youngsters were inside; three lads playing pool and an anxious looking girl. She stared at Gabi and Paddy with a mixture of animosity, hope, fear and aggression. Gabi nodded at Paddy, let go of his hand and entered the small room she used for her counselling sessions. She left the door open, put her handbag down, turned a small Tiffany-style lamp in the corner on and opened the window a bit to let in some fresh afternoon air. She heard Paddy in the hall. "Anyone for a brew or coffee?" Not even waiting for an answer he had already moved to the kitchen. There was no alcohol allowed on the premises, but the kids had free use of tea, coffee, water and refrigerated soft drinks. She heard one of the lads start talking to Paddy. A few moments later that same lad stood in the door with a mug of tea for Gabi.

"Paddy sends you this."

"Thanks Tom. How has your week been?"

"Alright Ms Gabi." Tom was 17, a bright lad, but already spending too much time in the wrong company; he had been on the verge of alcoholism, when Paddy started showing up in the club and simply chatting to the kids, not lecturing, but telling them about himself and how his addiction had caused all kind of troubles for him in the past. Tom now adored Paddy and spent more and more time either in the club or out at the beach surfing. "I was surfing with Nick yesterday!"

"And what do you think...how is Nick doing with his football legs on the surfboard?" Gabi took a sip of her tea and smiled at Tom.

"He actually is quite good." Tom looked down and seemed to try to look for the right words. He sighed.

"What is it, Tom? Is something troubling you?"

"Not me." He pulled a chair closer and sat down near Gabi. He started to lower his voice. "You saw the girl...she goes to school with me. Her name is Emma. She...I think she has trouble at home. I told her to come here and talk to you. I told her that you and Paddy are ace!"

"Thanks Tom, I feel honoured." Gabi grinned. "Well tell your friend Emma, that I have time to chat with her now, if she wants. Or we can arrange a time that is better for her." Tom nodded and got up. "Thanks Ms Gabi." He left the room. Gabi put a notepad and a pen on the little table and waited. Her policy was to let the teenagers come to her, rather than encourage them in. That way they really only came, when they were willing to share.

She heard Paddy laugh with the lads, while playing pool with them. When she looked up, there were two piercing green eyes staring at her.

Gabi smiled encouragingly. "Do come inside and take a seat, if you like. My name is Gabi."

The girl slipped inside the room and pulled the chair away from Gabi, before sitting down. She was very nervous.

"Tom told me that your name is Emma? Lovely name – I have a friend up North with the same name."

"I hate it."

"If you could choose, which name would you have?" Gabi openly looked at the pretty, slightly under-nourished girl with beautiful ginger curly hair. Pretending not to notice Gabi took a mental image of the bruises on Emma's wrists, the way she kept her legs closed tightly together and the fact that she was wearing long sleeves on a warm late summer's day.

"Don't know. Does it really matter?"

"Everything that matters to you is important, Emma."

Emma opened her eyes wide, and they showed the kind of pain and despair that you should not have to see in any child's eyes.

Emma laughed a toneless laugh. "No one really cares. I just can't bear it all anymore."

"Tom cares – he invited you here. I care and am happy to listen to you."

"What could you possibly understand? You have a perfect life, no one can force you to do anything you don't want." Emma's agitation turned into aggression.

Gabi moved her chair more into a 45-degree angle to Emma. "I have not always had the perfect life – and what may look perfect to you, is not necessarily all perfect. People see what they want to see."

"Well I am sure your man out there does not throw you on the kitchen table to...force himself in you." Emma swallowed hard.

Gabi took a deep breath. She wanted to say and ask a thousand things, but knew it was better to remain silent and let the girl part with as much as she could at this first encounter.


When they walked home in the lovely cooling evening breeze, Gabi was quiet. As much as she loved her counselling sessions with the teenagers, sometimes they really stuck with her. Paddy knew that she had something disturbing on her mind. He just pressed her hand while walking up the hill. Gabi stopped all of a sudden. "I can't do it, Paddy. I can't walk away from her tonight."

Paddy pointed at a wall nearby. "Let's sit down and see, what can be done."

"You know I can't talk about my cases…but I could really do with your support here."

"I gather that. No names…just facts, and you are not breaking any rules."

"One of the teenagers I talked to tonight told me that she was raped by her step-father."

"Did she give you her name and address?"

"I only have her first name. She seemed very nervous and distressed."

"No wonder. Did you report it?"

"Well…I only have half the story. She was spooked by one of my regular kids arriving and got up and left. I really only have bits and just put them together myself. She has not actually accused him or named him. I am just worried, she might harm herself. I need to find her."

"How?"

"Tom knows her. He might also know, where I can find her."

"Ok. Go back, talk to Tom, alert the authorities and have your back covered. I will go and get the car and meet you in the harbour car park. Then we can get to where we need to get to easier."

Gabi nodded, hugged Paddy and rushed back to the club. Tom was still there, playing pool. Gabi waved him outside.

"Tom, I forgot to ask your friend Emma something. Would you know, where I can find her?" She tried to sound calm.

Tom sighed. "Well she never really hangs out with us. Dunno really."

"Do you know where she lives?"

"Yeah, two houses above the gallery that always has these big paintings in the window." Gabi nodded.

"I have seen her outside the chippy near the graveyard a few times."

"Thanks Tom. Oh…what is her surname?"

"Portland, Emma Portland."

"That's great. Enjoy your game now." Gabi turned and started to walk towards the graveyard. She sent Paddy a quick text to let him know, where he could find her. As she got closer to the graveyard, she saw a figure against the glowing sunset huddled over one of the graves. Instinctively Gabi increased her speed. She entered the graveyard and approached the girl.

"Emma, it is me, Gabi."

The girl did not move. Gabi got closer and touched her tenderly. Then she realised that Emma was not going to move. Gabi tried to turn her round and saw blood dripping from her wrists and a razor blade on the floor. Gabi immediately tore strips of her cotton dress and wrapped them round Emma's wrists. She took Emma in her arms and got back up taking in the name and age of the man whose gravestone they were leaning against. She got her mobile out again and phoned 999. Paddy arrived almost at the same time as the ambulance. Emma was slipping in and out of consciousness.

"She cut her wrists, but horizontally. Still she seems to have lost quite a bit of blood....and I am not sure, if she has also taken pills!"

"Ok, we will take it from here. Can you give us some details?" Gabi did and then followed the ambulance with Paddy in the car.

"Good job you did turn around." Paddy put his hand on Gabi's leg.

"I really should not have let her go."

"Gabi, you saved her. Now you can deal with the rest."

"I could sense she was in serious trouble – I should have…"

"Shhhh Gabi. You have just saved that girl. Darling we are doing voluntary work here, and we are doing a damn fine job."

"Maybe…I think that her step-father abuses her…hence I found her on her dad's grave. The way she was talking, I would actually not be surprised, if there was more to it…"

"More??? Isn't that enough already?"

"It certainly is more than what a girl should have to cope with…however I think something pushed her over the edge. Because the abuse has been going on a while, judging from the scars on her arms and the apparent ease she opened up about the sex."

Paddy remained quiet while they approached the hospital and finally parked up. Then he turned to Gabi, before they got out of the car: "You think she is pregnant by her step-dad?"

Gabi sighed. "Something like that, yes."

"Oh goodness me…what a bastard!" Paddy put his arm around Gabi while they walked into the hospital. After a few formalities, they sat down in the waiting room. A doctor came in.

"Are you the parents of Emma Portland?"

"No. I am her counsellor, and this is my partner. We found her and called help."

"Oh, ok. Well then you know that I cannot really talk about Emma to you."

"We don't expect you to. We just want to make sure that she is going to be ok."

"Emm – yes. The wounds on her wrist were relatively superficial. But...."

"She is pregnant?!?"

"I cannot really talk about that. But...."

While the doctor was trying to find a way of saying something without giving away personal information, a couple burst in.

"What happened to my girl? Where is Emma?"

Everyone looked up and stared at the newcomers. The woman talking was very attractive and unnecessarily done up; the man looked strong and not older than 40. He had something unsavoury about him. Paddy got up. Gabi held him close.

"Are you Mr and Mrs Portland?" The doctor turned to the couple.

"Yes. Where is our daughter?" The doctor took them outside and talked to them.

Gabi nodded at Paddy. "Do I say something now or do I ...."

"Thank you for saving my girl." Mrs Portland came back in and reached out to Gabi. "The doctor says you found her and called the ambulance."

"Yes. I am a counsellor, Mrs Portland. Emma had been to see me."

"Fine job you did then!" Mr Portland aggressively pulled his wife back into the corridor.

Gabi closed her eyes and counted to 10. Then she approached the doctor on his way back. "Doctor, I need to alert you and social services about Emma. So where do you want to talk?"

The doctor nodded and led Gabi in his office. "I am Emma's counsellor. I know that her stepdad is abusing her quite violently....and I think she is pregnant by him."

The doctor put his head in his hands and sighed. "I thought something like that, when I examined her earlier. She has a lot of bruises and partly healed cuts. And yes, she is pregnant."

"Oh dear. What next then?"

"I will alert social services and they then will approach the parents. Emma will stay with us in the meantime."

"Can I come and see her?"

"I don't see why not. She might want to talk tomorrow. She is sleeping now."

"Ok. Here is my number…just in case." Gabi got up, gave the doctor her business card and left. Paddy was waiting outside and took her hand, as they walked back to the car.

They drove home with soft jazz playing on the radio. As they got in, Gabi excused herself for the evening and went upstairs to have a hot bath and early night. When she sat in the beautiful bath and took in the relaxing scent of lavender, she started to cry…that poor girl. Would she ever be able to enjoy the pleasure of being with a man?

"I won't offer you a penny for your thoughts, because I can imagine them. Here is a glass of your favourite wine." Paddy handed her a glass and kissed her lips.

"I really love you, Paddy."

"Of course you do – what is not to love?" He smiled and left her to relax.

When she came into the bedroom a little while later, her man was waiting for her. "Thought you might need a cuddle."

Gabi smiled at him. "A cuddle? Yes, for starters…."

3

They fell into a deep sleep in each other's arms. Gabi woke up in the early hours with a feeling of unease. She opened her eyes. All she could see was the moonlight flooding in, the curtains being moved ever so slightly by the breeze coming up from the sea and something else. She squinted and tried to see better. For sure there was a shadow in the corner of the room, near to the bathroom door. Her heart started beating faster. A part of her wanted to turn the light on, another part wanted to close her eyes again and not really find out what that shadow was, but rather cuddle up close to Paddy again who was sound asleep. The shadow did not move at all. In the end her curiosity got the better of her.

"Who are you?" she whispered into the direction of this shadow. "What do you want?"

While there was no response from the shadow, Paddy moved. "Why are you not sleeping, love? Are you ok?" Paddy sat up, and the shadow left.

"There was something in the room."

"What are you talking about?" Paddy switched the little lamp on his bedside table on. "There is nothing." Paddy got up and went to the bathroom.

"Paddy, seriously, there was something in that corner." Gabi got up herself and walked to the place where she had seen the shadow. She looked on the floor. "Look!" She pointed at a tiny puddle on the floor.

"Now, that is a bit weird." Paddy bent down, dipped his finger in the puddle and put the tip on his tongue. "Saltwater."

"Creepy!" Gabi started to shiver a bit. Before Paddy could say anything else, there was another big bang coming from somewhere underneath them. They looked at each other.

"We really need to find out, what is causing this bang. And we will need to find out a bit more about the history of this house, I guess...but for now, let us go back to bed. You are shivering, Gabi."

Gabi followed him and cuddled close to him. Her mind was racing. A ghost? Really? And why all of a sudden and never before? And this banging noise. And Emma. Paddy felt her restlessness and just started stroking her head very softly. The next thing she knew, there was sunlight in the room, a steaming brew on her bedside table and Paddy singing in the shower.

Gabi was sipping her hot tea and trying to make some sense out of last night's events, when Paddy came out of the bathroom, the towel wrapped around his hips. "Well, top of the morning to you! You are looking a bit perkier again." Paddy kissed Gabi and sat down next to her.

"Good morning to you, and thanks for the brew. You really know how to please a woman!"

"Do I now?"

"Mhm, yes you do! Perfect cup of tea...." Gabi put her mug on the bedside table and placed her warm hand on Paddy's leg, very slowly moving it upwards. "....and then the welcome sight of a handsome man only dressed in a towel...."

Paddy grinned and let her get rid of the towel and stroke his already erect penis. He groaned and started breathing heavier. Gabi pushed the bedcover aside and pulled her man inside the bed. They were in the midst of blissful love making, when a bang louder than ever before thudded through the house. "What the f....!!" Paddy tried to ignore the noise, but it returned, still louder. Annoyed he pulled out and got up.

Gabi looked at him and giggled. "The ghost has an absolute shit timing!!"

"Most certainly. Ok let's get dressed and check all this out. I definitely do not want to be so rudely interrupted again!" His lips closed around hers, his tongue exploring her mouth, making her sigh. Then he went back to the bathroom. Gabi smiled. This man in so many ways was one in a million; and every day she thanked the universe for having brought them together at a stage in their lives, when they both were truly able to appreciate the uniqueness of each other. She loved him with all her heart, but in a way, that was soothing for the soul, comforting for the mind, inspiring to her spirit and definitely blissful for her body. She got up as well, picked some clothes and then entered the bathroom, just as Paddy came out.

"I won't be long." She tenderly stroked his stubbly cheek.

"No worries, I will see, what the others are up to and what we are having for breakfast."

Gabi stepped into the shower and enjoyed the warmth of the water and the lemon smell of the shower gel on her skin. As she stepped out and started towelling herself dry, she felt as if she was not alone. However, she could not see or hear anyone. She stepped in front of the mirror cabinet to get her facial cream out, when her heart almost stopped. She was not looking at her own face in the mirror – the woman looking back at her had dark long hair that was tussled and looked soaked, her eyes were deeply brown and her whole complexion was more than just pale. Still it was clear that she was absolutely beautiful, but also incredibly scared. Gabi just stared at the face, incapable of moving. It was only the dog barging into the room that broke the spell. Millie growled.

Gabi bent down and stroked the dog. "It's ok, Millie, I don't think we need to growl here."

As she straightened herself and looked back in the mirror, she could only see herself...the other woman was gone.

As she came downstairs, she could smell the bacon and eggs, toast and coffee. Martha looked at her and Millie, while pouring coffee for everyone. "You two look as if you have just seen a ghost!"

"Maybe because we have!"

Both Paddy and Nick turned towards her. "Seriously now, Mum?!"

As she sat down, she told Martha and her son about the ghost in the night, and then all of them about the woman in the mirror and Millie growling.

"Cool! We have our own ghost!" Nick grinned, not quite sure, what to actually think of it all.

Paddy looked at him. "You and I will need to make sure that the women are safe here, when we are not around. So, after breakfast, we will see, what we can find in those caves to start with. And Martha...you have lived around here all your life. Are there any legends or folk tales associated with either the house or the caves?"

Martha sat down and took some bacon. "Not that I know. I mean of course there are all the smuggler tales and pirate stories, but this house is not all that old really."

"No, but the caves are. And what was here before this house?" Paddy poured milk in Gabi's coffee and passed the little jug around. "I really am intrigued now. Let us all go down into town later and talk to people. Someone is bound to know something, particularly the old folk."

"Exciting really." Gabi grinned. "I bought the house mainly for its stunning location and views, but now we have a secret to discover."

After breakfast Paddy and Nick made their way to the cellar. Again, they tested the thick stone walls to check for secret doors. Nothing. Paddy was not happy. "I am sure there must be a way down to the caves from here."

"Well we have checked all the walls...nothing moves, nothing even sounds hollow."

"Ah – but we have not checked the floor, have we?"

"Fair comment." Nick took his stick again and started knocking on the floor. Paddy used the big torch and looked for any clues on the floor, anything that could hint at a trap door. They found nothing. Eventually they looked at each other and went back outside.

"Let's go into town then, talk to the old folk and see, how we get on. There is always someone who knows something, and people love their old wives' tales and gossip."

Martha was just locking up, as they approached the house again. "I have to go to the shops. I will also talk to a few people. Gabi will join you later; she has driven to the hospital to see that young girl."

"Of course. Thanks Martha. We will nip down to the harbour ourselves now and see, if we can find out anything about this place. The walls in there are solid – no secret path from the storage cellar." Paddy was lost in thought, when they started walking downhill. He thought about the ghost, the apparition or whatever the woman in the mirror and in their bedroom wanted to be called. He really did not like the thought of leaving Gabi on her own in there. He knew she was not easily scared, but he also knew that the shadow in the night had unsettled her. He was a man of reason; he wanted explanations. And he knew that there would be a story to explain it all – one way or the other. Gabi had enough on her plate right now with that girl she felt responsible for.

"Emma, how do you feel?" Gabi sat down on the chair next to the girl's bed. Emma looked pale, but somehow more settled.

"I am ok, I guess."

Gabi nodded. "Emma, you are safe now. You can think about your future."

"The doctor told me that social services had been informed...I guess that has something to do with you?"

Gabi took a deep breath while checking Emma's eyes. "Yes, I suppose it has; with me and your doctor who was also concerned for your well-being. Yours and your baby's."

Emma reached for Gabi's hand. "Thank you. I did not really want to kill myself, I just wanted a way out. And I also hoped this might be a way of getting rid of his baby."

Gabi pressed her slim hand. "Emma, you need to get yourself better. And I am sure that social services will provide you with all the advice and support you need, when you make a decision about this baby."

"I don't want it. It is his. I hate him, I would hate the kid. And I want to go to university and not stay at home and raise a kid."

"I can understand that. I really can. And I think you are a bright girl. Does he know?"

"I have not told him. I only found out myself 3 days ago."

"Ok, just try and rest, eat and drink, get some colour back and then make a decision. There are of course various options regarding the baby. And there are also various options for how to go on from here. You do not have to go back home, but no one can stop you, if you want to. We did not get to talk about everything; where does your mum fit in in all of this?"

"She loves the bastard. She is besotted with him. God knows why."

"Does she know that he raped you?"

"I don't know. I tried to tell her, but she really does not want to know. And I sort of felt for her. I mean what kind of man rapes the daughter of the woman he is supposedly in love with?"

"Have you ever seen or heard him be violent to your mum? Judging by the bruises and cuts on your body, he has not been very tender or careful with you, has he?"

"Tender?? He usually waited until mum had gone to work or to the shops, then he pinned me down front or back on the kitchen table, pulled my pants down and forced himself in. He really hurt…I guess he has quite a big dick. Even when he had finished, I could still feel him inside of me for hours."

Gabi closed her eyes. She really hoped that he had not done her more physical damage.

"But mum, no I have never seen him hit her or anything like that. And according to the noises from the bedroom, she seemed to enjoy him."

"Emma, I will have to leave you now, because Social Services are about to come and talk to you. I leave my card on your bedside table. Do call me, if you need anything or just want to talk."

"Can you not stay? I don't really want to be on my own with them; I trust you."

"Ok, let me step outside and talk to them."

"Thank you…for everything."

Gabi smiled at her and went outside. The woman from Social Services had arrived, as well as a police officer. Gabi introduced herself and told them that Emma had asked her to remain present during the interview ahead.

"Have you been counselling the girl for a while?"

"No, I only met her yesterday."

"Well it looks like you are very good at your job then, if she trusts you so much." The woman from Social Services gave her an ingenuine smile.

"Of course, I would like to think so. However, it is quite common that in a crisis a patient clings to the counsellor. This girl has been traumatised for months by violent rape; then she has to find out that she is pregnant by her raping step-father. She seeks help and wants to get out of this situation, but she does not know how. So, she draws attention to her situation by faking a suicide attempt. She has not opened up to anyone else apart from me so far. So of course, I am the person she trusts, because in her mind I have saved her from the hell she was living in."

"And so you have." Doctor Houseman had joined them. "You found her, brought her to the hospital and alerted the authorities. She can now let go and leave the solution to others."

Gabi smiled at him.

"If you don't mind, "he addressed the two officials, "I will check on my patient. And then you can interview her."

4

It was already the middle of the afternoon, when Paddy received a text message from Gabi. He and Nick had spent the past hours chatting to people about the house and the caves underneath, trying to come across some kind of rumour that could explain the bangs and the ghost. They had split up; Paddy had finally settled in one of the nice harbour pubs with a coffee and a pasty, when he struck lucky talking to an old man who used to go out fishing, but had long since retired. He was one of those characters that know everything that is going on.

At first, he was quite suspicious of Paddy's Irish accent; but when Paddy bought him the second beer, things lightened up between them. Jago was the old man's first name – the Cornish form of James. He just started telling him about the caves that had of course been used by smugglers, when he all of a sudden seemed to remember something else.

"Now I come to think of it, there was this girl once....it must be a good fifty years ago, maybe even more, because I was just a young lad myself then. She was a stunner; all black hair, round figure, busty – well you know, the sort of woman you look at twice at least." He giggled. Paddy smiled and nodded encouragingly.

"I can't quite recall her name, but she used to meet someone in the caves. He was not one of the local lads." He gulped down the last of his beer and looked at Paddy. Paddy got up and went to the bar for another round. That was when Gabi's text message reached him. He let her know in response, where he was and asked her to meet him there. He returned to Jago and was greeted with an appreciative grin.

"Cheers me good man." Paddy smiled in response. "And what else do you remember about that girl?"

"She disappeared and was never found." Paddy nodded, urging him on. "I think her family lived somewhere up the hill. They were never able to bury her."

"Why do you think that something bad happened to her? She might have run away."

"Na – in those days girls did not run away from home. I think that man had his way with her and then killed her."

"But if he killed her in the caves, would the corpse not have been found? I mean, the caves are well visited by folk, and they are pretty accessible."

"The sea holds many secrets." Jago nodded to himself and concentrated on his pint. He seemed to have forgotten about Paddy. Luckily at that point Gabi entered the pub. She looked around, spotted Paddy and walked across.

"Good afternoon, gentlemen!" She kissed Paddy and sat down next to him with an expectant look.

"Gabi, this is Jago. He is a local fisherman and knows all there is to know about this place. Jago, this is my partner Gabi. She is an author."

Jago looked up. "What kind of books do you write? I can tell you some great stories." He smiled a seemingly toothless smile at her.

"I am thrilled to meet you, Jago. And I would love to hear some of your stories. I am particularly interested in everything to do with the caves and any other rumours or secrets relating to the house on top, which is where Paddy and I live."

"There are many stories. Will you mention me, if you use them in your book?"

Gabi thought for a few seconds. "I have just finished my last novel. Why don't I start a completely new book with your help? I am convinced that together we can come up with a great adventure."

Jago took that in. "My stories are not cheap, you know."

Paddy and Gabi exchanged a quick look, both trying not to laugh about the sudden change in Jago.

"I wouldn't have thought they are. If they are reliable local history, I am not only happy to mention you as my source and inspiration in my book, but I think you will be able to demand an upfront payment as well. And of course, a share of the royalties once the book is ready and being sold."

Jago put on a serious face. Paddy closed his eyes and chuckled to himself. Gabi knew she had Jago's interest and was already developing a layout for her next novel in her head.

"How much are you offering upfront? A man needs to live."

"Of course, Jago. Why don't I go home and phone my publisher, while you think about a suitable sum, and we get together again tomorrow evening. Join us for dinner, Jago."

Jago quickly licked his lips. "Very well, that sounds ok."

"Brilliant. See you tomorrow." Gabi got up, Paddy followed her. Outside the pub he turned around to Gabi. "You are not only going to talk to him about what could be behind the ghost and the bang; you are really going to develop the whole thing into another novel, aren't you?"

"And why not. Two birds....one stone..."

"Why not indeed. You look like you have achieved something? How is the young patient?"

Gabi took Paddy's hand and told him about her hospital visit and the less than pleasant conversation between the social worker, police and Emma. "Thankfully Dr Houseman was present as well. He is really good with Emma."

Paddy stopped and pulled Gabi round to face him. He looked at her. "I guess I know what you want to do next."

"You mean apart from kiss you?"

Paddy pulled her closer and locked his lips with hers, pushing his tongue into her mouth, entwining with her tongue. He could feel her starting to breathe heavier. She really was his little slave, no matter how successful, determined, independent and brilliant she was outside their relationship. He pulled away and smiled at her. "You are offering Emma to move in with us, aren't you?"

"Do you think that is a bad idea?"

"She will lean on you, possibly get fixated with you. However, you can give her love and understanding, and you can probably help her to get the education she wants while feeling safe. It is your call. She is vulnerable; you must make sure to strengthen her self-worth, give her space to lick and heal her wounds, but at the same time not allow her to wallow in self-pity."

"I know. And I have you by my side. She has touched something inside of me, and I want to help her to fix herself."

"I know. And you also want to mother the daughter you never had."

"Paddy! It is not...."

"Gabi, I can read you – never forget that. And there is nothing wrong with having different sets of motives, when doing something good."

"You think it is good then?"

"It is better than leaving her to it and making her face all the upcoming decisions on her own. Plus, I really do not like the look of her step-dad."

"Thank you. I love you, really do."

"I love you, too, my little slave." Paddy kissed her again and then continued to lead the way home.

5

Martha had filled the house with delightful smells of Cornish lamb, roasted vegetables, herbs and spices for the evening of Jago's visit for dinner. Thanks to it being a warm and very calm evening, the table was set outside on the veranda. It was also Nick's farewell dinner, before returning to university for the next few months.

Millie barked shortly, but then simply wagged her tail, when Jago was asked to come in. He was wearing his Sunday best – an old and well-worn suit, a clean shirt and a tie that had seen fashion come and go. He had clearly taken the time to even have a shave and shuffled his feet at the door to make sure, he would not be bringing in any dirt. Nick shook his hand and took him through to the veranda, where his mum and Paddy were already enjoying the stunning look out over the sea and their first drink. Both got up to welcome their dinner guest and smiled.

"Jago, welcome to our home!" Paddy shook his hand and Gabi gave him a brief hug.

"Can I get you a drink?" Nick looked at him questioningly?

"Well I would not say no to a nice cool drink."

Paddy smiled. "Get our friend here a Pennycomequick. I am sure that you are partial to a smooth local stout?"

Jago licked his lips. "Don't mind, if I do. Thanks laddie." Nick went off and soon returned with one bottle he handed to Jago and a few more of the same stuff in a cooler. He was followed by Martha who brought the dinner nicely laid out on a big platter. She nodded to Jago who in response grinned at her.

While Martha served everyone, Gabi looked at their guest encouragingly. "Please Jago, feel free to start telling us more about that girl. Have you by any chance remembered her name?"

"Yes, it was Emblyn." Martha nodded. "I have heard the stories of Emblyn – now that you mention it. Pretty 17-year-old Emblyn and the stranger."

"An unusual name." Gabi took a mental note of it.

"It is an old Cornish version of Emma or Emmeline." Martha handed the gravy round.

Gabi and Paddy looked at each other, both struck by the coincidence.

"So – what is known about the stranger? Was he really a stranger or did he disguise himself?" Everyone turned to stare at Gabi who blushed a little. "Well I am just wondering where and how would Emblyn have had the opportunity to meet a stranger in those days?"

Jago emptied his first bottle. "Well fair question. And I have never actually seen the man myself, only Emblyn."

"I only recall folk talking about Emblyn and a stranger, older than her. I am not sure, if anyone ever saw him close enough, because from what I heard they always made sure to meet at the beach near the coves either at sunset or dawn." Martha finally sat down.

They all ate in silence for a while, appreciating the delicious food and getting lost in their own thoughts about Emblyn and the man who clearly in one way or another had become her fate.

Then they started a lighter conversation on more current affairs in the town, leaving the more burning story for after dinner time. With coffee and brandy seated comfortably in the living room, Gabi finally steered the conversation back to young Emblyn and her doubtful fate. "So, what are the actual facts about Emblyn's disappearance, as far as people remember?"

"She was last seen on a relatively stormy evening, heading towards the coves. It was the night before her 18th birthday..." Jago had the voice of an old story teller now, everyone was hanging on his lips. "She must have been wrapped in one of those woollen shawls that women used back then. That shawl was the only thing left or found of her, when folk noticed she had gone and headed for the beach and coves to look for her."

"Nothing else... ever?" Paddy looked into the old man's eyes.

"No. It was as if she had disappeared from the face of this earth."

"That could also mean that that man took her with him to wherever he had once come from. And they could actually have lived happily ever after." Gabi smiled.

"No Darling, I don't think so. Something happened in those caves that night that was far from a romantic happy end. Otherwise we would not have the unsettled ghost of a young woman in the house now, would we?" Paddy poured some more coffee.

"No, I suppose not." Gabi put her hand on Paddy's and looked pensive. "I also wonder, why we had no apparitions before... would this be something like a special anniversary of whatever happened to her? Jago, do you recall what time of the year Emblyn disappeared?"

Jago scratched his head in thought. Martha put her cup down. "Well I actually do remember that it was indeed this time of the year, because we had gone back to school, when the rumours started."

"What I don't get is that no one seems to know anything about this guy. I mean, he must have met her somewhere local, he must have stayed somewhere to do so. This was in the days before internet dating, so people actually had to meet, before they could establish an interest in each other." Paddy looked at Martha.

"I was just a kid then. But you do have a point of course."

"Is there no family left? Did Emblyn not have siblings who went on to have kids?" Nick got up with his mug of coffee and walked to the big terrace door looking out over the sunset on the bay.

"Valid questions, my son." Gabi looked at Martha.

Martha looked at Jago. "Jago, I just remember folk talking about someone not belonging here. I really was too young. Do you not know more, since you remember Emblyn so well?"

Jago scratched his chin. "I seem to remember he was a captain from Plymouth. Emblyn's mother did not live too long after the disappearance; there was another daughter. She was sent to become a nun after these events. The whole family withdrew. They felt shame – it was all different in those days."

"Well I think we are stuck a bit with the story for now. And it is late enough; lets come to an end for tonight." Paddy got up and nodded at Jago. "If there is anything else you remember, Jago, you know where we are."

The old man grunted and got to his feet. He said his good-byes and trotted off home. Martha took the coffee cups through to the kitchen and tidied away, while Nick took his dog for a last short walk.

Paddy kissed Gabi's neck. "Come on, let's go. We need to think all this over and get some sleep. Ideally uninterrupted by ghosts and bangs in the rock." Gabi got up and followed him. He was already asleep, when she climbed into their bed. She cuddled up to him and was soon asleep herself, dreaming about handsome captains, young girls lost in love and someone watching in the shadows.

6

After an indeed quiet night with uninterrupted sleep, Paddy was up first. "Wakey, wakey, lazybones! Got to see your son off today, do some more ghost hunting and see to picking up your new child..." A quick kiss and Paddy had left to get his first coffee.

Gabi stretched and then got up for her morning routine. Breakfast was served, when she entered the big kitchen with their be-loved breakfast corner. "Good morning all...Martha it smells delicious, what have you been up to already?"

"Just some bacon and cheese croissants." Martha opened the oven door and the amazing smell filled the room and crept upstairs.

Paddy was reading the paper and about to finish his first mug of coffee. "I think we should have a walk to the actual caves later on." He folded the paper and put it away just as Martha put the fresh croissants on the table. Gabi took another sip of her tea and went back into the hall. "Nick, breakfast!"

"I really wish I could stay longer in order to help solve the mystery!" Nick was into his third croissant.

"I am sure you have enough coursework waiting for you at uni!" His mother was already in the process of helping Martha pack the prepared food for Nick to help him survive without the delicious home cooked meals he was used to every day.

"And girls to chase!" Paddy winked at him.

"I don't need to chase them, they flock to me like moths to a flame!" Nick grinned and got up to get ready.

An hour later they were on the way to the station. Hugs and good-byes were followed by waving and blown kisses, as the train pulled out of the station. Gabi sighed, Paddy kissed her. "He will be back sooner than you think"; he took her hand and led her back to the car. "Hospital next??"

"Mhm yes. Do you really think, it is right to take her in?"

"Darling, as her counsellor you should not form such a close bond – we both know that; however, as the wonderful caring human being you are, you have no other option...with it all out in the open now, the man would no doubt try and take revenge in one way or the other. She needs to feel safe, particularly while the police investigate."

"Thanks, my love – I needed to hear that. I will rather help finding her a different counsellor in order to be able to offer her a safe haven with us."

"Of course. You are you, and I know that you still feel responsible for having let her walk out of the youth club. Really though you have saved her life and made sure the bastard was exposed. So, let us pick the girl up, let her settle in and then take her for a nice walk to the caves – give her something different to occupy her mind."

"I really do feel blessed and immensely grateful for my life as it is today. You are simply perfect for me."

"If you say so." Paddy smiled and drove to the hospital. It was not in his nature to talk too much about feelings. And thinking back, it had taken him much longer than Gabi to appreciate that their chance meeting indeed was the beginning of something amazing, a relationship simply perfect in so many ways. He was absolutely content with his life now. Gabi gave him all her love, she was his intellectual partner and always good for stimulating conversations, she was funny, she was confident and successful, she was loving and caring, accepted people as they were and always tried to do good by everyone. Most importantly she let him be without trying to change him and without questioning him. There was no jealous streak in her. She accepted his need to be out with his mates or simply on his own. He had tested that beyond the limits of what women normally accept, and she had never given him a hard time. When she decided to purchase this house in Cornwall with her phenomenal royalties from the movie they had turned her first book into, she only asked him, if he would come and see her still – now that she would be much further away from him. That actually was, when he realised that he had been trying to not see her as much as he could have, because he had not wanted to really be tied into a relationship again. All of a sudden though the thought of Gabi possibly leaving his life again became too much to even consider. So, he proposed to buy this house together, sell his own and make a proper go of things; and he could not be any happier. He now loved coming home, feeling part of a family again, enjoying the life they had built up together. He even contemplated giving up his job in Real Estate and just doing the counselling. Life was beautiful, time precious. Their life was so in balance and harmony; yes, maybe it was time to stop all the rushing around. He parked at the hospital car park.

"You were deep in thought during the drive." Gabi stroked his hand that was still holding the steering wheel.

He turned around. He was not going to tell her his decision at this point. "I love you more than I ever let you know." He whispered more than spoke out loudly, and then he kissed her the way she desired to be kissed.

"Wow." Gabi gasped for air. "Whatever brought this on, we should have more of that more often!"

"Let's go and get our girl!" He looked at her and the deep love in her eyes. Yes, his decision was right.

Hand in hand they walked to the hospital entrance. Just as they were about to enter, a man blocked their way. "I guess it is you we have to thank for interfering in business that has nothing to do with you!!" Next to him was Mrs Portland in tears.

"Good afternoon to you, too." Paddy looked him straight in the eyes and thus let him know that he knew exactly, what kind of man he was.

"They are not letting Emma come home with us."

Gabi took a deep breath. "Mrs Portland, would you like to sit down and talk over a cup of tea?" The woman looked at Gabi, blew her nose and seemed to think.

"The fuck she wants to talk to you!" Her husband pulled her along. "This is not the last you have heard from us."

"Most likely not. We will probably see you at Court!" Paddy turned away and took Gabi's hand again.

While the Portlands left the hospital with him cursing and swearing, Paddy squeezed Gabi's hand. "What a low-life."

"To be honest, I just hope that she has the strength to kick him out and as time goes by build bridges with her daughter. "

"Doubtful that – she must have known, and she still carried on shagging him. I really don't get it...and I just hope for her sake that he is now not going to turn violent on her."

Dr Houseman waited for them in his office. He briefed them on the conversation with Emma's parents and then listened to Gabi's proposal.

"To be honest, I am glad that you are offering to take the girl in. I did not really want to hand her over to Social Services; she needs love more than anything else, and a safe place to lick her wounds and make some tough decisions about her future. Physically she is ok; well I dare say that she needs some pampering and some decent food."

"Martha will see to that." Gabi smiled. "I will of course suggest for Emma to see a different counsellor. Is there any paperwork we need to fill in, anything we need to sign?"

"Emma turned 18 today; so she can legally decide, where she wants to live."

"Oh that is brilliant; shall we go and talk to her then?"

"Please do. Just come back for a check-up next week, and of course, if there is anything else that you need medical advice with."

"Thanks Doctor." They shook hands with the doctor and went to Emma's room. She looked so forlorn in her hospital gown, almost as white as the sheets.

"Hiya!" She instantly smiled, when she saw Gabi. "Thanks for coming by."

"Well, my dear, we are here with a suggestion. You have briefly met my partner Paddy, haven't you?"

Emma nodded. She looked at the Irishman and tried to weigh him up.

"Pleased to meet you, Emma. Gabi and I wondered, if you feel strong enough to leave the hospital."

"I am not going back there. Not ever!"

"Of course not, Darling." Gabi put her hand on Emma's thin arm. "We would like to offer you to come and stay with us, at least until you have decided, what you want to do with your life, where you want to go, and what will happen to the baby."

Emma stared at her, then at Paddy. She swallowed hard. "Really? You would do that?"

"If you want, you can get ready now and come home with us."

Emma's eyes filled with tears. "I can't believe this."

Gabi just took her in her arms. Paddy nodded and went outside. "Emma, you will be safe with us...and we will look after you, if you let us."

Emma nodded, sniffed and hugged Gabi back. "Thank you so much. I promise to be good."

"Oh Darling, you are good – and we will love having you. Let's get sorted and go."


Within half an hour, Emma was ready to go. She signed the paperwork for the doctor and carried her little bag of stuff that her mum had brought her the first night. In the car, Paddy rang Martha on hands free.

"We will be with you in about 15 minutes. Is everything ready?"

"Of course, Mr Paddy. The room is ready and aired, dinner is in the oven and the afternoon tea will be on the table, when you walk in."

"What a jewel you are!"

"Nonsense. Did Nick get off ok?"

"Oh yes – see you soon!"

A short while later they parked outside their beautiful home. The late afternoon sky was play of colours to behold. Emma stared at the Manor House, the surrounding trees and the view over the Bay. "Are you sure?"

"We are very sure." Paddy took her bag, Gabi put her arm around her. "Prepare for Millie, the family dog."

As Martha opened the door, Millie escaped, jumped at Paddy and then circled around Emma. She sniffed at her and rubbed her head against Emma's legs.

"She likes you and knows that she needs to treat you carefully!" Gabi smiled at the dog and then led Emma inside.

"Tea is on the table. Some scones as well."

"Thanks Martha. So, this is Emma who will now be living with us; and this is Martha without whom this household would not function."

Emma put her hand out so shake Martha's. Martha just pulled her close and gave her a hug. "Have a brew, and then we will get you sorted in your room."

7

Emma walked around her new room, touching everything. It was so beautiful. Bright and light, warm colours throughout – it had been the guestroom of choice, now it would be Emma's. Within the house it was next to Nick's room; like his, it had an en-suite shower and toilet. The view was into the stunning countryside. In the window there was an integrated window bench – something Gabi really loved, and Paddy had made sure to have that fitted in all the bedrooms.

"Is there anything you need right now?" Gabi appeared at the open door and smiled at Emma. "I will take you shopping tomorrow – after all, it is your birthday today, Dr Houseman told me."

"You have already done so much!" Emma smiled with utter happiness. "This is all so beautiful...and you and Paddy...thank you..." She closed her eyes.

"You deserve it, my dear girl. Now put a cardigan on and come for a walk with us. The fresh air will be good for us all, and Millie will definitely enjoy the walk."

Emma looked through her bag, but there was really just some underwear, toiletries and a PJ. "I'll be fine!"

"It can get quite breezy. Let me get you one of Nick's jumpers. He won't mind, if it is worn by a pretty girl like you." Gabi went next door and took one of Nick's Cashmere jumpers out; it was dark green, which really complemented the young girl's complexion and hair colour. Together they set off downwards to the harbour and then to the coves. Paddy helped the ladies over the slippery stones separating the town from the rocks. Emma needed a few seconds before feeling able to put her hand in Paddy's. He only held her hand lightly and talked to her in his soothing voice about the banging they had heard recently, and how they were now on a mission to find the source of it.

"I used to go to the caves for peace, when...I needed to be alone."

"Did you ever notice anything unusual?"

"No – I loved the fact that most people do not really venture inside and explore the tunnels. I did."

"Tunnels??" Gabi and Paddy asked at the same time.

"Yes, I only found them by chance really. About a year ago. That day he had...been particularly painful. So, I wanted to make sure that for the rest of the day I would not have to be alone with him. I planned to hide here until it was time for mum to be home. And just before I arrived, it started to rain. A group of the surfers also seemed to be heading for the caves. So, I ran and got there first. And because I did not feel like talking to anyone, but could already hear their voices, I moved further and further back. Then I realised that right in the left-hand corner there was a sort of draught. A narrow passage lead on. I quickly stepped in and followed it."

"Wow, no one else has actually mentioned any tunnels to us so far."

"It is a bit of a labyrinth really. I kept coming back and ventured a little further every time. I even created a map."

Gabi put her hand over her mouth. "Right, do you remember, if any of those tunnels lead upwards?"

"Most do. The smugglers must have used them in the olden days."

"Girl, you are a Godsend for sure!" Paddy took a deep breath and seemed to be coming up with a plan. "Do you still have that map?"

"No. I got scared that he might find it and follow me. I do remember most of it though."

"Well, what a successful walk this turned out to be!" Paddy spontaneously hugged and kissed Gabi. "Tomorrow we will get the girl kitted out with decent walking shoes etc, and then we will come back with torches and sketchpads."

"Good idea. For now though, let's start the way home, have a shower and get ready for Martha's culinary delights."

Just as they got home, the house phone rang and was answered by Martha. "Oh good to know! ... Yes, they have just returned...hold on, I pass you on to your mum...and look after yourself!" With that Martha handed the receiver to Gabi who had a brief chat with her son, while the others scattered about. Millie's feet were cleaned, before she got her food in the kitchen. Emma looked around unsure of what to do. Paddy sensed her eagerness to not put a foot wrong.

"Emma, if you want to go and have a shower before dinner, now is the time. We will do the same as soon as Gabi comes off the phone. You really can move around the house as freely as you like...and if you need anything at all, just ask one of us. Also, if you want a drink, let Martha show you where everything is. Don't feel like a visitor, girl. This is your home now."

Emma looked at him. His face was weather worn with sparkling blue eyes; he had clearly gone through some rough patches in his life himself. Yet he seemed to have such an honest calmness about him, an almost tangible kindness. In spite of herself and her weariness of men, she nodded and gave him a quick hug, before dashing upstairs to her room.

Martha handed him a cup of coffee. "You charm everyone, you do!"

Paddy smiled at her. "Martha, that is a very nice thing to say. Good job you did not know me 10 years ago."

"We all have faced our challenges; it does not matter, where we come from, it matters who we are now and where we are going. And you are spreading love and kindness."

"Don't you start now, Martha! Womenfolk and their wet flannel talk!" With a sheepish grin Paddy gave Martha a kiss on the cheek and went upstairs. He was just adjusting the water temperature in the shower, when Gabi joined him. Her full breasts rubbed his back.

"Mhm – kind of massage I like!"

Gabi got the shower gel and started gently massaging it into his skin. When he turned to face her, his erection tickled her belly. He took the shower gel off her and returned the favour until her quiet groaning told him that she was ready to welcome him.

Giggling they came out of the bathroom with towels wrapped around, when there was a shy knock on the door. Gabi quickly checked that they were decent and then called out: "Come in". Emma opened the door a little and asked: "Just checking...will it be ok, if I wear my PJs for dinner? I am so sorry, but I do not have my clothes here and did not want to put the others back on."

"Emma, all that matters, is that you are comfortable. In fact, we will all wear some leisurely clothes tonight. Don't worry about things like that at all."

"Ok, thanks. I shall see you downstairs in a few minutes." She left again, closing the door firmly behind her.

"She seems to be a really nice kid. I hope that we can help to heal the damage that evil bastard has done to her. I might nip to the police station tomorrow and see, how they are getting on with the case. After all, you do not really want me around, when you go clothes shopping?"

"They will probably not tell you anything anyhow – still, it doesn't hurt to let them know, where they can find her now. And I shall think about, where to take her for some clothes that is not too far."

8

After a successful shopping trip to Falmouth Gabi and Emma returned with plenty of bags to unload from the car. Paddy helped them carry everything inside.

"Wow you really have gone to town!"

"Just a few things a girl needs!" Gabi grinned at him. "Oh, and there is a present for you, too."

"Ah now, that is very nice of you." Paddy opened the bag and pulled out a beautiful salt and pepper coloured fisherman jumper that was really soft to the touch. "You shouldn't have! But it sure is very much appreciated. It is just the sort I like."

"I know, Darling! You will look great in it – I am sure you must have been a sea captain in a previous life!"

Emma chuckled and started taking her bags upstairs. She looked happy. While she was unpacking all her stuff and arranging it in her wardrobe and chest of drawers, Gabi sat down in the living room with her man. Martha brought fresh tea in.

"She looked really pleased." Paddy poured tea for everyone.

"Most girls love shopping for outfits – Emma is no exception. And we had a few good chats. I think we did the right thing in getting her here."

"And we will have to make sure, she gets through this trial. With the statements from the doctor, yourself, social services and Emma, they will have to take him to court. And they want to do it as soon as possible. It will not be nice for her – he is going to make out that she lead him on etc. I know his kind. And we don't know, what the mother is going to say."

"Might it be worth, me going and trying to talk to her?"

"Not sure, love." Paddy rubbed his head. "She seems to be smitten with him; and Emma not wanting to go home, will have hurt her in some way, I guess."

Gabi nodded silently. "Rape cases are always unpleasant. Still – we know the truth and will stand by her."

"We will also need to talk about the baby at some point."

"Yes. You know that I am not a fan of abortion, never have been. However sometimes it seems to be justified. It is not, as if she just fell pregnant by her boy-friend. She says that she would hate the child as much as she hates him. And that is no blessing for a new life to enter this world, is it?"

"Very difficult situation." Martha herself had always wanted children, but had had three miscarriages. "Somehow, I think that, if not conceived in love, children face a difficult, somewhat cursed fate."

"She is of age anyhow. She can and must make her own decision." Paddy got up and looked out over the Bay. Clouds were gathering. The sky was of a strange blue-grey with a touch of doom looming. He turned around, when Emma entered, dressed in jeans and a dark green, figure hugging silk shirt that really made her eyes glow. Her hair was tied in a long pony tail. She really was a little stunner. And she looked at him with a shy smile. "What do you think?"

"Beautiful! I wonder, if you have some Irish blood in you!"

"Come and sit with us, have a brew and a biscuit." Gabi patted the place next to herself. Emma sat down. Paddy watched her and realised that there was only a fine line between admiring a pretty young girl and feeling drawn by that kind of Lolita into more inappropriate desires. Still the man was her step-father, that alone should have kept him under control. Temptation though...

A very loud bang stopped him in his trail of thoughts. "Like a sign from above!" he thought to himself and couldn't help grinning. Emma looked startled.

"These are the infrequent bangs we were talking about yesterday." Gabi took Emma's hand. "My conclusion is, something or someone is trapped in those tunnels underneath and want us to set it free."

"Agreed. We do need to find the connecting tunnel between those caves and this house. Even though we have not found anything from up here, there must be something. Emma, when you were exploring them, did you come across anything that even remotely suggested a blocked door or passageway?" Paddy got up again.

Emma looked into the distance, thinking. "I can't say I did."

"Right, shall we wrap ourselves for the weather, put some firm shoes on, grab paper and pencil and start on tunnel trip number one?" Paddy moved towards the hall. Millie followed him expectantly.

"Ok. I shall get my waterproof jacket and boots. Emma, please make sure, you wear decent shoes for this. We don't want you to slip or trip over and hurt yourself or the baby."

Emma pursed her lips. "I don't really care about...it!"

"But we care about you. So let's get ready, before it starts pouring down. The clouds are gathering." Gabi stroked the girl's shoulder and went upstairs.

Emma looked up and locked eyes with Paddy which prompted another loud thud that ebbed through the rock. "Gabi cares for you, Emma. We all do. Please help us look after you. And we really need your help down there in the caves."

Emma kept looking at him. "Yes. I shall get the right shoes and the rain jacket."

When she had gone upstairs, Martha took a deep breath. "You need to be careful." She said quietly, while putting the tea mugs on a tray.

"Not to get lost in the caves?" Paddy smiled at her.

"That as well. But you can always leave a trail of breadcrumbs like Hansel and Gretel...I think..."

"Shh!" Paddy gave her a little hug. "I am not stupid, Martha. I know what you mean. Don't worry. My desire is elsewhere. And I am aware, which also means that I am prepared."

"Good, I am glad to hear that. You might still want to take a little backpack with old bread!" Martha chuckled now.

Paddy grinned. "Do you not trust my pioneering skills, woman? I was a scout once!"

"Just keep your head about you."

Paddy nodded and got the big torch from the hall cupboard. Soon they were all outside with Millie excitedly leading the way.

9

The sky had gone to various shades of grey, promising rain. They walked and chatted about a multitude of other things rather than the strange appearances in their home. When they reached the cave, Paddy handed Gabi the big torch and Emma the pad and pen he had brought.

"Right ladies, this is the plan: Gabi walks ahead with the torch, Emma behind mapping the way. I will be at the end – obviously safeguarding the ladies."

Gabi looked at Emma and burst out laughing. "I like the chivalry, Paddy; however, I do not expect any cave trolls to attack."

Emma smiled. "I never really felt uneasy in here, when I did my exploring."

"You can laugh now. I did bring my Swiss army knife in any case."

Millie barked not knowing what was going on. As they started moving again, she decided to stay in the back with Paddy. The darkness ahead was not really her thing.

They gave it a good 2 hours of exploring the various tunnels. None of them so far seemed to lead far enough up to be able to reach the house. It was starting to get cold, and Gabi started yawning. "I think I have had enough for today. Shall we had back?"

Emma agreed. "I think I will put my notes and scribbles into proper maps, when we get back. Then we can see, what we have actually covered today."

"Right ladies. Fair comment. I really am amazed at the labyrinth down here. This must have been smuggler's heaven at some point. Anyhow, let's turn and head back."

Millie wagged her tail enthusiastically, when she realised that they had finally decided to leave this cool and unwelcoming tunnel system. As soon as they reached the cave exit, she was off, racing along the beach, chasing seagulls and barking happily.

"I get the impression, our dog was not as excited about this little adventure as we." Gabi picked up a piece of driftwood, whistled for Millie and then threw it, when she returned. She did that a few times. Emma sat on a rock and watched. Paddy sat down next to her. "Are you ok, Emma? This was not too much for you, I hope?"

"No. I am a good walker. Just sitting here and watching Gabi with Millie, makes me remember, what a beautiful part of the country this really is. And I am ever so grateful to Gabi for saving me."

"A heartfelt yes on both accounts. And Gabi is definitely one of a kind. She knows, what she wants. She can be very stubborn as well; however, there is no better woman in this world than her. She gives so far more that she has ever received. Without doubt she is the best thing that happened to me – and I am not ashamed to admit that."

"What do you have to admit?" Gabi had just re-joined them.

"Now I am not sure, you need to know that." Paddy got up and hugged her.

"Fair comment. Everyone needs their little secrets. Shall we get going? That cloud there looks like it wants to burst over us!"

Emma lead the way with Millie at her heel. They had not even reached the streets again, when the heavens opened indeed. Heavy rain was soon followed by thunder and lightning. When they finally reached home, they were all drenched. Millie shook herself frantically and was not all too happy, when Martha caught her in her big towel.

"Hold on, young lady. You are not bringing all your dirt into the house. And you need a rub anyhow!"

Gabi, Emma and Paddy left their shoes by the door, took their jackets off and looked expectantly at Martha.

"Of course, there is fresh tea in the kitchen. And dinner will be ready in about 45 minutes. So you have plenty of time to get changed into something dry and comfortable. And...did you find anything?"

"Not yet, Martha." Paddy poured tea in 4 mugs. "Emma is going to draw up a proper map of what we have explored today."

"I really did not expect there to be so many tunnels down there." Gabi grabbed her mug and warmed her hands on it.

Emma looked at everyone. "I am wet and a bit cold; still I am happier than ever in my life. I am so grateful to you all. This is what family should be like."

Gabi put her mug back down, pressed one in Emma's hands and kissed her on the forehead. "You are part of this family now. And we are happy to have you."

Emma's eyes filled with tears. She looked at Paddy and nodded. "You are right." Then she grabbed her stuff and went upstairs to get changed.

Martha looked at Paddy enquiringly. He just grinned. "Come on, light of my life, let us nip upstairs and put some dry clothes on. You look like a water rat!" Teasingly he kissed Gabi on the cheek.

"Thank you very much. Did I ever say that you are a charming Irish man?"

"Too many times for me to remember..."

"Seriously, Martha, why do we bother?" Gabi had already finished her tea and placed the mug next to the sink. At that moment an enormously bright flash of lightning illuminated the view to the back-land – and in it Gabi clearly saw a woman in front of what looked like the ruins of an old stone building. "Did you see her?" Martha picked the dog's bowl up for cleaning.

"Who?"

"I saw a woman out there." Gabi was already at the door shining towards the bushes and bracken with the big torch. Nothing. Millie sat down next to her, followed the direction of the torch light with her eyes and growled.

Gabi closed the door again, stroked Millie's head and just stood in the hall for a few minutes.

"Are you ok?" Martha addressed her and, thus, brought her back to reality.

"Yes. Sorry. Maybe I am starting to see things...overactive imagination; might come with the territory of being a writer. I will go and have a quick shower now – something is already smelling good."

"That is the pork in cider. Paddy loves it."

"Beautiful. Just the sound makes my mouth water. I shall be quick." Gabi went upstairs. As she entered the bedroom, Paddy who was sitting in the bay window with his eyes in a magazine looked up with a smile. "What kept you, love?"

"Our ghost. Emlyn. She was outside the kitchen window. Well not directly, but a bit further in the back between the bracken and bushes."

"Really? She is getting a bit incessant."

"Mhm." Gabi rubbed her forehead with one hand. "There must be a reason."

Paddy got up. "Of course. She wants her secret uncovered and the culprit exposed. And she knows that you won't let it rest." He took her hand away from her head, held it in his and kissed her forehead. "You will have to up your super sleuth skills."

Gabi smiled. "Paddy, I might take you for a walk to the hinterland tomorrow." With that she went to her wardrobe and picked some leisure clothes to change into after her shower. "I fancy a juniper and tonic tonight."

"Your wish is my command." Paddy left her to it and went downstairs to get the requested drinks ready. "Fancy a non-alcoholic Gin and Tonic, Martha? Or do you prefer the real thing?"

"Actually your version is just as tasty, so I shall have that. Is Gabi ok again? She looked sort of spooked before."

"She is fine, Martha. The sooner we get to the bottom of all the ghostly going-ons here, the better though. Anyhow dinner smells great; life really is great."

"So it is." Martha smiled.

<u>10.</u>

The next day started with heavy rain. So they postponed their planned walk to the hinterland. Paddy busied himself on his laptop with research, and Gabi took Emma to the living-room.

"Darling, we need to talk about your future."

"I know. I really do not want this baby. It is something that would tie me to him forever. just could not love it. If that is bad, then I will have to be bad." Emma looked at Gabi with tears in her eyes.

"Emma, you are not bad at all. And your thoughts are not bad either; in fact, they are very mature. I totally get it, believe me. You have various options of course, even if you do no want to care for the baby yourself."

"Yes, I know. I just do not want to give birth to it. Sorry. I really want an abortion."

"And then? What are your plans?"

"College is done. I did not send off any applications to universities; I am not sure. My hea was so messed up all these months...years really. I did ok with my grades, but I could hav been much better."

Gabi leant back on the sofa she had chosen to sit on. She felt for this girl, she really did. Sh wondered, if men who rape children really fully understand the complete damage they do the utter violation of a body and soul. Of course Emma was messed up. And even thoug Gabi in general was against abortion, in this case it really seemed the best way. Emm needed a chance to heal, to grow into a woman and learn to love and trust again, before sh should contemplate motherhood. Emma may be a young adult in years now, however tha man had stolen her girlhood and taken all the sweet innocence, all the excitement c discovery of the other sex and her own sexuality from her. Emma really was a girl trapped i the body of a pretty young woman. Gabi just pointed at the empty space next to her. "Com and sit with me."

Emma got up and sat close to Gabi. Gabi put her arms around her and held her. Emm started sobbing. She really needed to let go of all the strenuous negativity inside of her. Ga just held her and stroked her back, while Emma cried and cried. Eventually she stoppe Gabi passed her the box of tissues from the little table next to her.

"Sorry." Emma said quietly.

"You really have nothing to be sorry for. This was well overdue, Emma. Tears clear the soul like shears clear the garden after a long winter – that is an old Japanese saying, and I quite like it."

"Will you help me?"

"Of course, Emma. When the rain clears, we will take Millie for a nice walk. Then we phone the hospital and ask for an appointment with Dr Houseman for tomorrow. He will advise you on the whole procedure."

"Can you come with me?"

"Emma, I will go with you, wherever you want to be accompanied to. You should also look for a new counsellor."

"Why? I can talk to you."

"Yes, you can talk to me. I cannot be your counsellor anymore though. It would be unprofessional."

"I don't understand that."

"We are too close. As a counsellor I would have be take a more neutral stance and not be so emotionally involved with you."

"Oh. Ok. Do I need counselling, if I have you?"

"Yes, I think you will need counselling to work through the months, the years of abuse. And don't worry; I am still here for you as your motherly friend."

Emma embraced her. "Thank you so much. I shall never forget, what you have done for me, what you are doing."

Gabi smiled. "When you have the abortion behind you, we will look at the various options for your future career. When your head is free again, you will be able to start thinking about things you can see yourself be passionate about. That is what a career choice should really be based on."

Emma nodded. She did not really know, what she would like to do with her life. She certainly was not going to depend on a man like her mum did. Maybe that was unfair, but she really wanted to make sure to always have her own income. She enjoyed drawing, she loved Art. Maybe that was a direction to take.

Millie came in wagging her tail to let them know that it really was time to go out for a decent walk. Emma cuddled the dog. Gabi got up to check on the weather. It had indeed stopped raining. However, the colour of the sky promised more rain to come.

"Alright Millie. We will have a brisk walk. Emma, do you want to come or rather stay in the dry?"

"I might go and take a nap actually. I feel a bit sick and faint."

"Yes, no surprise there. Get yourself comfy, and if you need anything at all, Martha will look after you."

"Paddy!" Gabi called upstairs. "Do you fancy a walk with Millie and me?"

"Coming!"

Gabi and Paddy sat off in wellies and waterproofs with Millie leading the way. They walked hand in hand.

"How did it go?" Paddy asked.

"She wants an abortion. So I shall take her back to the hospital tomorrow to talk to Dr Houseman."

"Yes. It probably is for the best…Millie, what are you doing there?" The dog had come to a halt and was intensively sniffing at a pile of rocks, taking a scent and then following it a bit further to one of the ruins within the bracken. Millie circled the area excitedly. Finally she stopped abruptly and howled.

"Good grief, girl. That must be some exciting scent!"

Gabi stopped as well. "This is about the same spot, where I saw the woman yesterday evening."

Paddy took a deep breath, let go of Gabi's hand and looked around the area, where Millie sat expectantly. He looked around the walls that had not collapsed, pushed gravel and dirt about with his wellies, but could not see anything of interest. He looked at the dog. "What is it, Millie? You may smell something, but I cannot see anything."

It started raining again. Paddy looked at Gabi and shook his head. "Come on Millie, lets get a bit more walking done, before we turn back." He bent down to pull her away from the spot she seemed to be rooted to. Millie shook herself free and started digging.

"Well Paddy, she definitely has something there she wants to unearth!" A few moments later you could hear the paws thumbing on something that was definitely more solid than the mud around. Paddy bent down and used a stick to prod the hole that Millie had dug.

"Wow. This is metal. I wonder, if this is the opening to one of the mine shafts."

Thunder and lightning put a stop to their investigation for now. Rain started pouring down again. Millie quickly went behind a bush to do her business and then dashed off home. Gabi knelt down next to Paddy. "If this is an opening to the tunnel system underneath, we could possibly find the source of the banging from this end."

"Yes, and God knows what else." Paddy got up again. "Let's go home. This will have to wait for a drier day. And it might need proper securing." Gabi looked at him. "What a story!"

11

Dr Houseman sat down with the two women. He had examined Emma to make sure that all was well with her and the baby.

"Emma, you may not look it, but you are a strong and healthy young woman. All is well with you physically, and with the baby."

"Why do other women who really want a baby have miscarriages? And this one hangs on???" Emma's eyes filled up.

Gabi looked at Dr Houseman, thought briefly about her own struggles for falling pregnant so many years ago, just took the girl's hand and started: "There is no justice in this world. There are a lot of things that make you wonder, if there is a God...still I like to think that everything happens for a reason. Let's not think about why you are still pregnant; let us just find the best solution for you without harming you and your future chances for falling pregnant again."

Dr Houseman smiled at Gabi with a grateful look in his eyes. He was glad, she had replied to the girl's question. Now it fell on him to explain the procedure.

"I agree with Gabi, let us focus on the task ahead. If you are entirely sure that you want to go ahead with the abortion, since you are under 9 weeks' gestation, my recommendation is the following: I give you Mifepristone today. You go home. The day after tomorrow you come back and I give you the second pill: Misoprostol."

"Can I not have both in one go?"

"Yes that can be done; however it is safer and more effective to do it with a gap between the two."

Emma looked at Gabi who still held her hand. "Emma, let us go with what Dr Houseman suggests. It is not a problem for us to come back in 2 days."

"Good, "the doctor continued. "The first pill sort of prepares your body. You might get nausea and vomiting as a result of taking it, and you might not. If you have to vomit within the first hour of taking the pill, you need to come back and we have to give you another one."

"Ok, no change there. I feel nausea more often now anyhow."

Dr Houseman smiled. "The second pill will be inserted in your vagina. I can do that or you can do it yourself at home – whatever you find easier for yourself. That second pill will cause cramps and heavy bleeding, usually for a few hours. You will need pain killers, and we will also give you antibiotics. The actual abortion will show up as large blood clots, as the sac with the foetus is pushed out. It will at your stage be smaller than a normal grape. Most women pass the pregnancy within 4 to 5 hours after taking the Misoprostol. However you might continue with some kind of bleeding for up to 4 weeks afterwards. That is normal. And I would like you to use sanitary pads to track the progress. Do you have any other questions?"

Emma took a deep breath. "No. I can understand all that. And thankfully I have Gabi." She pressed the older woman's hand really hard now. She would not admit it, but of course she was scared of the whole process. And a part of her felt like she was about to commit a really sinful thing.

Gabi smiled at her. "As long as you are sure that this is, what you want to do, we will both support you all the way."

Emma nodded. Dr Houseman busied himself with preparing some paperwork. Then he handed her the first pill and a large glass of water. "Emma, remember; if you start vomiting within the hour, you need to come back. Otherwise, I shall see you the day after tomorrow."

As they got home, Martha was busy in the kitchen. Paddy sat in the living room talking to one of his clients on his mobile, while jotting down some notes every now and again in his leather-bound note book – a present from Gabi.

"Martha can you please make Emma one of those herbal teas you prepare, when one of us has a bit of an upset stomach?"

Martha looked at Gabi, read her thoughts and rummaged in her herbs and spices cupboard. She produced a glass jar containing yarrow. She put the kettle on, got a big mug out and a normal sized one.

"Emma, how do you feel now? Do you want to go upstairs for a nap or stay downstairs and have company?"

"I might go upstairs for a bit. Sort my shopping – well all the different exciting pads and maybe just put the TV on."

"Ok, my love. Make sure you are comfortable and let us know, if you feel poorly or need anything. Martha's special tea will help." Gabi hugged her and watched her go upstairs. Paddy appeared in the kitchen. "And??"

"We have started phase 1. And the day after tomorrow we are going back for the second one; and that one will induce the abortion."

Paddy only needed to look at her once to see that this was just as hard for Gabi as most likely for the girl; different reasons of course, still he could sense that Gabi was not all at ease with all this herself. He kissed her head and started to massage her shoulders. She sighed and leaned in on him.

Martha smiled. "I shall take Emma's special tea upstairs and make sure, she is ok. Your mug is here, Gabi. Normal green tea for you."

Thanking Martha, Gabi grabbed her mug and followed Paddy into the living room. They sat down on the big sofa facing the big window overlooking the bay. Paddy held Gabi in his arms, while she silently sipped her tea.

"You are doing grand here. I know that you are not a fan of the whole procedure; honestly though in these circumstances, I think the girl is doing the right thing."

"I know. And I feel for her in every way." She took a few deep breaths and closed her eyes enjoying the feeling of Paddy's body behind her. "I also know that you are about to tell me that you have to leave tomorrow."

Paddy chuckled. "Why do you say that?"

"Because even though you are a very warm and caring man, you normally only shower me with that much attention, when you try to appease me, because you need to tell me something that I might not like to hear."

"Oh Gabi. You are a one off!"

"Of course. And how long will you be gone?" He had always been very vague with his time commitments to her.

"Not more than a couple of days."

"Standard answer." Gabi put her mug down and turned to face him. "You better make every minute count that we have left until then!"

They were in the midst of passionate kissing, when a loud bang alerted them. "No..." Gabi sighed and let go of Paddy unwillingly. He smiled and continued to hold her close. Another loud bang that seemed to vibrate through the house brought Martha into the hall, Emma out of her bedroom and Millie pressing herself against Martha's legs and howling.

Paddy closed his eyes briefly and got up. He looked outside. It was raining heavily. "Really there is nothing we can do about that hidden entrance until we get a dry day. I think that ghost does not like me! Every time I want to get passionate with you, it starts this!"

Gabi chuckled. "Not every time luckily. As you say – there is nothing we can do right now. So let us try to carry on with whatever we all were doing."

Emma appeared in the door. Her hair looked tousled, her eyes were heavy. "Can I stay down here with you?"

Paddy took a deep breath and smiled. "Of course you can. How do you feel?"

"Very tired and somewhat queasy and dizzy. But not too bad actually for now."

"Martha's tea. It really helps." Gaby got up as well, grabbed a cosy blanket and put it over Emma. "Anyone for a cuppa?" She was already on the way to the kitchen, when the house phone rang. She answered. "Hallo?!"

Martha went back to the kitchen to put the kettle on. When Gabi joined her, she seemed somewhat unsettled. Martha looked at her, while preparing the different mugs. "Who or what was it?"

"A very faint female voice. And all she said was: help me!"

12

The next morning saw Paddy set off early. "Gabi, promise me that you are not going to try and get into that mine shaft without me being here! You will have your hands full with Emma tomorrow anyhow. And you need to focus on preparing your own upcoming trips. And..."

Gabi pulled him close and kissed him. "I promise. And you be careful on the roads and then let us know, when you have landed in Lisbon!"

"Ok. Will do." He had already started the engine and was about to leave, when he wound the side window down and waved for Gabi. She walked over to the car and put her head through. "I love you, Gabi. And I mean it."

"I love you, too, Paddy." Another kiss and he was off.

Emma and Martha were standing in the doorway. "That is the kind of relationship I want one day." Emma said quietly.

Martha put an arm around her. "Yes, they have something special."

Gabi joined them. "What do we do with this day? It looks dry."

"Everywhere will be soggy though." Martha shut the door.

"How about going into our little town, having a stroll through the harbour and lunch down there. I also think that the "Gallery on the Corner" has some new paintings. Are you with me?"

"I love Art. Yes please." Emma was the first to be ready. They put Millie on her lead and set off. The fresh air did them all good after more or less having been cooped up in the house for the last days. They watched the fishermen on their boats, Millie happily chasing seagulls and then chose a small Italian restaurant at the harbour front for their lunch. The proprietor knew Gabi and Martha, welcomed them with kisses on their cheeks and picked a nice table for them. He looked with interest at Emma.

Gabi noticed that. "Giovanni, this is Emma who lives with us now."

He looked at Emma and tried to place the face. Then he just gave up and smiled at her. "Buon giorno, Emma." He handed them all the lunch menu and disappeared.

After a lunch with plenty of salad, fresh fish and cool drinks and a well-behaved Millie under the table, they strolled back upwards to the gallery. Martha continued homewards with Millie, while Gabi and Emma entered the gallery.

The two looked around the exhibition. Gabi noticed that Emma was also looking with interest at the painting materials on offer. "Do you paint, Emma?"

"Yes. Well obviously not as fine as any of these paintings, but I love it."

"Have you done any oil paintings before?"

"No, just water colours really. They are at home...I mean, at my mum's."

Gabi left her to browse and went to find the owner of the gallery. In quiet voices they talked for a little while and then shook hands. Gabi returned to Emma.

"Emma, please get the materials that Richard here will pick for you. And then you can see how you get on with trying them out at home, before starting Art classes with Richard next week – that is, if you want to."

Emma turned around and looked at Gabi. Richard, the owner and local painter had joined them. "I would really love that. I enjoy painting. I love working with colours."

"That is a good start. I hear that you have not worked in oil before. Not everyone has to, of course. However, if you want to try, we can work together. Maybe you take a small canvas with you and just try something."

Emma nodded. She let Richard pick all she needed to start. Gabi paid for the material and upfront for the Art classes. She enjoyed being able to just buy something in order to put a smile on someone's face. That was the true joy of her wealth; finally, she was in a position where she did not have to count every penny to just make sure she had enough to buy the necessary grocery. She could just buy now without thinking. And if the truth were told, she did not really splash out on luxury items or fancy stuff for herself. Apart of course from the glorious house she had found and bought with Paddy. She just loved being able to treat the people she cared for. Emma hugged her. "Thank you so much, Gabi. You are amazing!!"

Gabi blushed. She had never been good with accepting compliments. "Just see how you get on. And if Richard sees potential in you, you might want to consider an Art College. The RCA is one option – and a very prestigious one at that."

Emma looked at her with bright eyes. Richard smiled and packed everything in a paper bag.

"I have put my card in there as well. We can start when you are ready next week."

Emma nodded and took her bag. Her mind was already on the best subject for her first oil painting. She did understand the basics of how to work with oil, she took one last look around the gallery for inspiration and ideas. Gabi all of a sudden went straight to a picture Richard had painted. "That is stunning. Where is it?" The painting showed a row of brightly coloured three-story houses, a church in the background, all reflecting in the light of a shiny river leading up to a pretty bridge.

"Oh that...I painted that many years ago during a visit to Ireland. It is..."

"...Cork!" Gabi smiled. She remembered the scenery from one of her visits with Paddy to his home town. It really was well done.

"Indeed. I am happy to see you recognised lovely Cork."

"I should. My partner is from Cork. This is beautiful, Richard. Is it for sale?"

"Mhm I am not sure. Let me think about it. It reminds me of a happy time with a proper Irish lassie." Richard got lost in his own memories. Gabi smiled at him. "No hurry, Richard. If you do consider to sell it, please let me know. It would be a lovely present for Paddy!"

With that the ladies left and started to walk uphill. Emma was chattering away about painting. As they got home, she immediately went upstairs to get pen and paper for a sketch of what she wanted to do.

As the evening settled down over the Bay of St Ives, Gabi and Martha sat in front of the big window with a glass of wine. Gabi looked into the sunset and smiled. Paddy had sent her a message telling her that he had arrived safely in Lisbon and was now out for dinner with a client.

"You miss him already, don't you?" Martha said with a glance to her friend and employer.

"I do, yes. Not in a painful way though. He just has become a pivotal part of my life, particularly since we moved together."

Martha nodded. She still missed her husband whom she had lost to cancer almost 5 years ago. They had also been very close; more so maybe due to the fact that they could not have children. Millie sensed a certain heavy mood in the two women and crawled between their legs. She put her head on Martha's foot and looked up. Martha smiled at the dog. "It is alright, Millie. We are just reminiscing."

"Would you believe that it took me almost a year to get Paddy to admit to his feelings?"

"Astonishing. He seems to worship the ground you are walking on, Gabi."

Gabi laughed. "Really?? He found excuse after excuse to not meet up; he drove me mad, made me upset with his behaviour. And then I realised that he was simply afraid."

"What of? Being loved by an amazing, kind-hearted and truly talented woman?"

"He was afraid of admitting to himself that he, too had already fallen in love and was wanting the closeness he shied away from. I did give him all the time he needed, and sometimes asked myself why I was letting him get away with his troublesome behaviour. All I wanted and needed was someone to hold me every now and again, someone to make me feel loved and wanted. I did not want to put shackles around his ankles...I just wanted his company every now and again, feel his touch and enjoy his presence."

"Men can get afraid of commitment, when they have been hurt and moreover feel like they have hurt and let down someone before who at some point meant the world to them."

Gabi looked at her. "Yes, Martha. I think that was the key issue in his case. And to be honest, if I would not have announced that I was moving away, I wonder, if he would not have continued to keep his distance to a degree."

Martha petted Gabi's hand. "Not important anymore. He lives with you now, and he loves it. He loves you with all his heart and soul. You two have something very special."

Gabi sighed and took a long sip of her Merlot. "Yes we do. He will always be my trouble, though...a bit like an Irish fairy."


When she stretched out in their bed alone that night, she chose Paddy's cushion to sleep on. It smelled of him. She fell asleep with a big smile on her face. And she woke up in the early hours, because her body sensed that something or someone was trying to touch her. When she opened her eyes, she looked straight into very blue eyes in a very pale face. Her heart stopped a beat.

"You have to help me!" The voice was hardly audible. And the touch she had imagined was more like a cold draught.

"What do you want from me?"

"You have to help me." The voice was even fainter, and the apparition became luminescent and then disappeared completely. It did leave a certain coldness in the room though and a strange smell. The distinct odour of moist walls, seaweed and something else, something sweet. Gabi sat up and switched her bedside table lamp on. Her heart was still beating fast, even though she really did not feel threatened at all. She took a long sip of the cold green tea that she had in her favourite mug on the bedside table. She listened into the silence of the night; the house was still, everyone asleep. With a smile on her face she got up. As soon as her feet touched the ground, she retracted them again; yes, there was another little puddle on the floor. Avoiding the puddle, she got to her feet and went to the bathroom to get some paper to mop it up. When she was back in her bed, she felt far too alert to go to sleep again. She wished Paddy was there to talk about this. The temptation to call him was enormous. She decided to instead send him a text message that he would find, when he got up in the morning. Blessed technology.

## 13.

The mobile phone woke her up. "Top of the morning, my love!"

"Good morning, Paddy. Are you ok?"

"Of course I am. Just saw your text. So what of your nightly visitor?"

"Only what I texted you. She asks for help. We must get to the bottom of this as soon as possible."

"We will, when I am back. You have enough on with Emma today. Good luck for that – to both of you!"

Gabi sighed. "Yes, we will have a difficult day or two, no doubt. Enjoy your customer meeting. Love and miss you!!"

Paddy smiled. "Love you, too." As he put his phone down, he started thinking. Being away from Gabi really did not hold much attraction anymore. He used to enjoy all his business travels; he still did to a degree. Missing out on time at home...home?...yes actually home however was not worth it. He had wasted far too much time in the first year of knowing Gabi. And he knew that it had really been almost too much time of circling around his own commitment issues, his fear of allowing someone into his life again competing with the desire to be with Gabi and giving it all a chance. She had told him much later that while he was trying to make his mind up and keeping away from her, she had met a man who was the total opposite, ready to start a new life with her; and she did like that guy and spending time with him. She was on the verge of going for it, when Paddy luckily got his act together and appeared at her door that all important evening. And the rest, as they say, is history.

He got up, made himself a coffee and decided that this was his last project. He also decided to propose to Gabi. She said, she did not bother about getting married again; he did not really himself. Still, there was something inside of him that wanted him to take this step. She was perfect in her imperfectness; she had from the very first day accepted him and his past addiction, his long months of indecisiveness, she was the most caring and giving person, he had ever met, she was sexy and intelligent, successful and devoted – yes it was only right to put a ring on her finger.

Gabi looked at Emma who was all pale this morning. Clearly anxious about the next step the termination of her pregnancy. She had no appetite.

"Do eat something, your body needs strength. How about a slice of toast and some fresh fruit?" Martha insisted.

Emma tried a little smile. Then she burst out in tears. "I feel bad for doing this."

"Now, now." Martha hugged her. Gabi took one of her hands. "Emma, you really have nothing to feel bad about, my love!"

"I am murdering my own child!" She sobbed relentless now.

Martha sighed deeply and went to put the kettle on again. Gabi nodded at her and then pulled Emma closer to herself. "Listen, sweetheart. Being the lovely girl you are, you were bound to have doubts when it came to the actual act. I do believe, you thought about this long and hard. We talked about it. Of course you can stay pregnant and have the baby; then you can keep the baby or give it up for adoption."

"I am sinful!"

"Emma, sin does not come into this at all from your side. You are considering the right step for yourself, your mum and the future child that will always connect you to your step-father. Do you need more time to think? Do you want me to call the hospital?"

Emma remained silent. She stared into emptiness.

"Emma, would you like me to phone your mum and ask her to come and talk with you?"

Emma shook her head slowly. She swallowed a few times. With a grateful smile she took the mug of herbal tea Martha handed her. "No, I can never talk to mum about this...or him. And I do not want a constant living remembrance of that man. There is a little part of me who thinks of the baby as a little copy of myself; the bigger part of me though will always see him in it. I could not love the baby. No, I cannot carry on with this pregnancy. I want to be myself, find out what I can do with my life; I want to make something. And then I want to meet a nice guy and have babies with him...I will still be able to have babies later, won't I?"

Gabi had tears in her eyes; she felt so sad for Emma and the tormenting decision she had to make and live with. Life could be so cruel. "You are healthy and young; I don't see why you should not be able to fall pregnant again, when the time is right for you. Do talk to Dr Houseman, before he inserts that pill, if you want to go ahead with it."

Emma nodded, took a little bite of toast and then peeled a banana from the fruit basket. When she had finished her breakfast, Emma went back upstairs to get a jumper. She felt chilly.

Not much was said during the drive to the hospital. Gabi felt somewhat sick herself, while she then waited for Emma to come back out of the consultation and treatment room. After what seemed an eternity, Emma emerged. Dr Houseman behind her just nodded to Gabi. "Phone me anytime, if you need me."

"Thanks Doctor." Gabi put her arm around Emma and led her to the car. When they got home, Emma went straight upstairs. Gabi looked lost.

Martha just looked at her. "Why don't you take Millie for a nice, long walk. I am here and will keep an eye on Emma. You look like you need some fresh air yourself."

"I think I do. Thanks Martha. Call me, if you need me." With that she whistled for Millie and sat off on her walk down to the harbour and then along the sea front. As always in upsetting times, she took great comfort from walking along the sea, looking out to the horizon and silently communicating with the universe. Millie enjoyed running and chasing seagulls. The sun started to set, when she got home. The fire was lit in the living room, an old movie was showing on TV and Emma was curled up under a blanket on the sofa. Martha saw to Millie and handed Gabi a cup of coffee.

"It is gone. She has lost it. I think the worst is over. She just needs our love now." Gabi went into the living room and sat down next to Emma, who instinctively put her head on Gabi's shoulder and stayed close to her for the rest of the evening.

14

By the time Paddy came back home, Emma had recovered well from the abortion. She had colour in her cheeks and was even putting on a little weight. All in all, he had been gone a little over a week; Gabi had met with Jago and started work on her new novel, Emma had busied herself with painting – she had done a few watercolours and was now working in oil. Her Art mentor Richard seemed impressed with her.

Paddy had brought a little present for the three women, and for now he kept the bigger present to himself. The engagement ring he had bought was safely hidden in one of his pockets; and he had not told Gabi about his decision to hand the business over. He just smiled to himself. His plan was to be really cheesy and ask Gabi's mum for her permission to marry her daughter. Their planned trip to Germany was only a few days away.

"I am getting the iron door in the bracken opened and the opening secured. So hopefully we can find something more, before setting off to Germany or upon our return," Paddy announced at dinner.

"The good thing is, none of us feels threatened by the banging or by the ghost of Emblyn." Martha served chicken and small roast potatoes, while Paddy handed the green vegetables around.

"Yes. I think we just need to find a clue to what happened to her and thus set her ghost free."

"We will get there, without doubt. Will you two be ok for the five days Gabi and I are gone?"

"Of course." Emma smiled with a newly found confidence. "We have to look after Millie and the house, and of course there is work to do with Richard."

"If you carry on at this rate, we will soon have to organise the first exhibition!" Gabi smiled at Emma.

"Ha, that will still be a while off. I need to learn so much more and improve my style. I really love it, though."

"It won't harm for me to have a chat with my old friend in Berlin who owns a gallery there. We will be there for the speaking and coaching for 3 days, before moving on to see the family. So, one evening we can meet up with him over dinner."

"Good idea. Does he already know, you are coming?"

"Funnily enough, he has seen advertising for my speaking event and got in touch on Facebook. We will also have to see my cousin for the other evening. Shame you have not improved your German much yet, Paddy."

"No worries. I know what I need to know." He chuckled to himself, and the women looked at him, then at each other with raised eye brows.

"What are you on about?"

"You will see, when the time is right."

Getting the iron door open was not a big problem; however, securing the entry into the caves proved more difficult. Paddy decided rather to be safe than sorry and told the builders he had employed to take all the time they needed. The day of departure came. Martha and Emma waved Paddy and Gabi off. Eurowings took them from Plymouth to Berlin in a little under 2 hours; they arrived in the late afternoon, took a taxi to their hotel, freshened up and went back out to soak the atmosphere in.

"I have been to Berlin many years ago," Paddy said, while taking Gabi's hand. "Yeah, but you were not with a German…so you did not really know, what to go for, what to look at. Apart from the obvious tourist attractions like the Brandenburg Gate and the Reichstag. I know we will be going for dinner later, but lets just share a Currywurst." Gabi stopped in front of one of the street vendors near the Brandenburg Gate and ordered a Currywurst. They stood at one of the tables and used their little plastic forks to eat.

"Mhm – fast food German style!" Gabi laughed. "What do you think?"

"I like it. Nice tang to it. Of course the best sausages come from Ireland!!" Paddy grinned.

"Not sure which sausages you are referring to!" Gabi winked. "If it is Richmonds…well…give me a nice Bratwurst anytime."

"Nick loves them!!" Paddy took another piece of sausage. "Just saying!"

"Yeah – now he is not really a culinary expert, my son!"

They carried on, strolled past the Gedaechtniskirche and finally reached the gallery that Gabi's friend and short-time lover of many years ago owned. He was waiting for them.

"Gabi! You look great!" He hugged her close.

"You don't look bad yourself, Wolf." She smiled. "This is my partner, Paddy." The two men shook hands. "What type of Art is your thing, Paddy?"

"To be honest, I am not very knowledgeable in Art. I see something and know, whether I like it or not…" he looked around, and his eyes rested on one of the latest Digital Art exhibition pieces. It was a picture from Manfred Mohr's Klangfarben-Series that had actually won a few Art prices. "I can tell you that I really like that one…the colours really seem to speak out to you, or even scream."

Wolf raised his eye brows. "Well this actually is one of the masterpieces here…and it is about the sound of colours."

Paddy smiled. "Not bad my taste then."

"Not at all!" Wolf said with a glance at Gabi who was actually beaming at Paddy. "Anyhow, let's go for dinner."

Gabi and Wolf briefly caught up with each other's lives and then discussed, what could be done for Emma. Wolf promised to contact some people in his network in England. They enjoyed some regional food and then said their good-byes.

"Will we see you tomorrow at Gabi's speaking event?" Paddy asked.

"Oh yes. I have bought a ticket and intend to learn something more about the Secret to Happiness."

"Great – see you then!"

While they were walking back to the hotel, Gabi asked "What did you think of Wolf?"

"Nice, smart, knowledgeable and pleasant guy. However, he clearly would have preferred you to be here on your own. And I for one don't blame him."

"I don't think so!"

"It doesn't matter. I am the one who is taking you to bed tonight."

"Mhm – is that a promise of some special fun?"

"Oh yes!"


After a relaxed breakfast the next morning, they went on to the museum island Berlin, as Gabi wanted Paddy to visit the Egyptian Museum, and particularly see beautiful Nofretete. Then after a coffee outside they got back to the hotel to get ready for the early evening speaking event at the prestigious Adlon Kempinski. The speaking event was held in German; however, Paddy was going to be in the front row just for mental support. Gabi loved it, when he could accompany her; even though by now she quite enjoyed being on stage and talking to as well as interacting with the audience, she still loved being able to see him, feeling him in the audience. Unlike other big speakers, Gabi did not usually travel with an entourage of staff. She delivered her speeches to an audience that had bought tickets online and could then order her books and subliminal tapes on-line as well. She preferred it this way rather than expecting people to buy her tapes and books there and then on the spot. Maybe not the best sales strategy, just her way of dealing with people.

What she really loved was passing on coping strategies; hence her speaker events were more like counselling sessions for big crowds. And people usually really took to her; they could feel the empathy behind the smartly dressed woman. Tonight's topic was all about "bringing happiness back into your life". Including Q & A her events usually lasted around 2 hours. Paddy listened to the rhythm of her voice, only understanding the odd word. He looked around the audience and saw they were loving her. Some people had brought copies of her books that they would ask her to sign. He looked back up and met her eyes...they spoke of love, utter happiness and joy of being alive; he felt really proud of her. Everything she had achieved, she had achieved on her own, holding on to the deep faith in her that she would get where she wanted to be. He smiled at her; she had brought out the best in him too. And his lifelong restlessness had disappeared. He knew now where he wanted to be and he was grateful for that. Standing ovations for his woman brought him back to the here and now.

She smiled, bowed humbly and took his hand to climb down the stage. People came to the front with their signing and selfie requests. Wolf was amongst them. He shook Paddy's hand and then kissed Gabi on the cheek. He handed her a piece of paper with names and contact details for Emma – true to his word. And then when the crowd finally disappeared, one couple came forward. Gabi beamed and rushed towards them to hug them tightly. Paddy waited in the background; he guessed this must be her favourite cousin Gerd with his wife Susanne.

"...and this is my Irish lucky charm, my inspiration and twin soul – in short, this is Paddy!" He smiled and shook the big hand Gerd held out for him, and then hugged Susanne briefly. "I have heard so much about you two!" Over the course of the evening, the two men bonded even though they both only knew bits of the other's mother tongue; Gabi translated effortlessly all the time and still enjoyed the regional specialties they had ordered in a small local restaurant. They laughed a lot and there were tears, when they said their good-byes very late at night.

"You must come and see us in Cornwall!" Paddy insisted.

"We will, promise. And you two remain good to each other – you make a great couple." More hugs, and then the taxi took the Germans home. "I now totally understand, why you love them so much. They are without doubt the most charming couple I have met in a long time!"

"So they are. Gerd has been the older brother all my life that I always wanted to have. I really am glad that you two hit it off...even through the language barrier."

"Sometimes language is not an obstacle, my love; communication happens on many levels.

"It sure does. Now let us get some sleep, because tomorrow will be another long night with my sister!"

"All good – and you were brilliant tonight. They absolutely loved you...I would not be surprised, if Viv would phone you next week to tell you that there was a sharp increase in the sales of your tapes!"

"Thanks. I am always at my best, when I can feel you in the audience."

"Wet flannel talk!!"

The next day took them to the Southwest of Germany, where they intended to spend 3 days with the family. This was only the second time Paddy was meeting Gabi's family. They were picked up at the airport by her brother-in-law Klaus.

"Well hallo you two! It has been a while!" He hugged Gabi and shook Paddy's hand. As soon as they got to the house, Gabi's sister Frederike rushed down the stairs to meet them. She had prepared a lovely light dinner and baked a beautiful chocolate cake for afters.

"So how was Berlin?" They were relaxing in the living room, every now and again interrupted by Peter and Frank, Gabi' s nephews.

"A real success, I dare say. Gabi is a natural on stage. People love her...she got standing ovations."

Gabi blushed. "Are you two joining for the event in Stuttgart tomorrow?"

"Of course. Mum as well."

"Lovely – it is comforting to have familiar faces in the audience. Gerd and Susanne send their love as well, by the way."

They caught up with recent events, and of course also talked about Emma and Emblyn.

"So we will meet Emma then at Christmas?"

"Yes – unless she decides to move on." Gabi smiled.

"Hardly!" Paddy put his mug down. "You are providing her with the safety, security and love that she has been craving in the past; that girl is not going to leave in a hurry."

"You really have a big heart, sis!" Frederike refilled her sister's glass and her own. The men took the family dog for a late walk.

"Now quickly tell me how things are with you and Paddy...I have to say, he is so relaxed now and definitely sooo in love with you!"

"And you would judge that by what, Frede?"

"By the way he looks at you, talks about you and seems so at ease with himself."

"All I can say is: I am so grateful that I followed my gut instinct and waited for Paddy to be ready. He is so worth the wait – in every way!"

"I can't tell you how glad I am to hear that. You have finally arrived – in so many ways. And he is such a charmer. God bless Ireland and the Irish!!" The sisters giggled and then lost themselves in some mutual childhood memories.

The next day took them for a nice country walk and then an early afternoon with Gabi's and Frederike's mum Ursel. At 80 years of age she was still fit in every way; she still missed her husband who had sadly passed away a few years ago, but she was determined to remain independent and self-sufficient for as long as possible.

"Gabi, you look great, my child!" She held her older daughter close. "It looks like your Irishman is looking after you very well." Ursel gave Paddy a hug, too.

Paddy smiled: "We look after each other. It is good to see you so well and healthy, too." After coffee and cake the traditional German way, Paddy insisted on helping Ursel in the kitchen to do the washing up. When they had finished, Paddy gently urged Ursel to sit down on her favourite kitchen chair, from which she usually observed the going-ons in the neighbourhood.

"I would like to ask you a very important question – which may come as a surprise to you."

Ursel looked at him. "What is it, son?"

"Unfortunately I did not have the pleasure to meet your late husband, otherwise I would be having this little conversation with him. Gabi is very much a family person, like myself. I would therefore like to ask your permission to marry your older daughter."

Ursel smiled. "Oh now, I really did not expect this. Have you asked her yet?"

"No of course not. If I do something, I do it right." Paddy smiled back at her.

"It looks to me like you two make each other happy. And you have embraced Nick in your life, too. I think that it is not necessary for you to get married; however I will certainly give you my permission. And I know that her father would have loved to see her so happy again – he always worried about her giving people, men and the world more than she got back. It looks like that has changed." Ursel got up and embraced Paddy. "When will you ask her? I am not very good at keeping a secret, you know!"

Paddy laughed. "I know, she keeps telling me that. After her event tonight, when we are all out for dinner."

"I might just be able to hold my tongue until then."

After another 2 hours on stage at the prestigious Graf Zeppelin Hotel at Stuttgart speaking, answering questions and being very focused, Gabi once again took Paddy's hand to step off the stage. A few people asked for signatures and selfies. Gabi smiled and happily granted both. She also looked at her man who seemed uncharacteristically tense. Her eyes asked him, what was wrong. He just looked back at her with a nervous grin. When the last people had gone, she pulled him aside.

"Are you ok, Paddy? You look...somewhat uneasy."

"No need to analyse me, counsellor." He tried to make her laugh.

"Paddy, I know you; and I know that something is making you feel uneasy. Fair enough, if you do not want to talk about it right now. Just that much: is there anything I can do to help?"

He nodded with a big smile. "Yes, in a little bit. Come on now – you are far too clever for your own good. Your family is waiting. Let us go for dinner."

"Mhmm...why do I get the impression that something is up?"

Paddy shook his head, kissed her, took her hand and lead her to the back, where her family was waiting. Off they went to a beautiful, rustic restaurant on the way home. They indulged in some local specialities. When everyone had finished, and they were just relaxing with an espresso, Paddy looked at Gabi's mum and smiled. He moved away from Gabi on the bench, briefly put his hand in his pocket and then the closed fist visible on the table.

"Gabi, in the presence of your family – apart from Nick who unfortunately cannot be here tonight, instead though with your mother's blessing I want to tell you that you are my soulmate, my best friend and the woman I really want to grow old with. I love you truly, madly, deeply...would you do me the honour..." he opened his hand and extended it to Gabi with the sparkling engagement ring visible to everyone ," ... will you marry me?"

Gabi stared at the ring in his palm, then at his face. In a thousand years she had not expected this. Her eyes filled up. She swallowed. Everyone stared at her waiting for the reply. She took the diamond ring in her right hand and brought it to her heart, then she smiled the biggest smile ever and nodded. "God, yes Paddy. I did not think that I would ever marry again. And I am not sure, what brought this on. However, I will be damned, if I don't take you up on your offer!" They hugged and kissed.

Then Paddy put the ring on her finger and smiled at her mum. Both Gabi and her sister looked at Ursel: "So you knew, and did not say anything?"

Ursel beamed at her daughters. "As you can see."

Klaus ordered a bottle of champagne to cheer the happy, now engaged couple. "Well Paddy, the Irish charm seems to really work. I am amazed to see my sister-in-law really going to tie the knot again."

When they were alone in bed later on, Gabi rested her head on Paddy's chest and asked: "What made you do this, Paddy?"

"I am not quite sure; I just know that it felt like the right thing to do. I am also retiring from my job. I want us to be together now; time is precious, and my time should be spent with you and doing the counselling – basically enjoying life with the woman I love. Problems with that?" He was stroking her short hair, while talking.

"I am utterly happy. And I relish the thought of becoming and being your wife. I did not think that I would seriously want to be married again. Been there, done it. You however put a new and exciting spin on everything. You have added to my happiness in so many ways." She started kissing his chest and worked her way down his belly to just above his now erect penis, when they heard steps on the wooden stairs leading up to this guest room in her sister's house. Giggling they quickly covered themselves.

"Auntie Gabi, can I see your ring? Mum told us that there will be a wedding soon!" Her little godson came to the bed.

Gabi smiled at him lovingly. "Of course you can, Frank." She lifter her hand and let him look at it.

"Wow. I bet that was expensive!"

Paddy was going to answer, but Gabi bet him to it:" It probably was; however the real value is in the fact that it symbolises Paddy's love for me. And now back to sleep, you little rascal. I am sure, your mum does not know that you crept up here!"

"No of course not. Night night!" And off he went.

Paddy locked lips with his fiancée. "That was very close! We better behave and sleep now."

"Indeed. Too much excitement for one day!!" Gabi laughed and snuggled up to her man.

<u>15.</u>

When they arrived home, they were welcomed by excited barking and heavenly smells from the kitchen. Martha hugged them both and then looked at Gabi's beaming smile enquiringly. Paddy grinned and took the luggage upstairs.

"Martha, we have a wedding to plan."

"Oh my God, is that so?" Martha looked at Gabi again, her eyes now wandering down to her hand with the engagement ring on it. She took the hand in hers and smiled at Gabi.

"I really am happy for both of you...and also for Nick. He likes Paddy."

"True. And he seemed genuinely happy, when we phoned him. Where is Emma?"

"She is out painting. She will have something to tell you, too. The police have been in touch; it looks like he is getting off."

"No. That is impossible."

"I am afraid so. He is a snake, and he made her out to be the Lolita seducing him, having been the one to initiate it all."

"I am disgusted. Then how do they explain the cuts and bruises?"

"Apparently she likes it rough."

"And then why would she now report him?"

"Because he was uncomfortable with it all, felt guilty towards her mum who he really loves and adores. He really had an answer for everything."

"How did Emma react?"

"She just throws herself into her painting. And she has decided that she needs to leave, because she does not want to have to face him anywhere."

Gabi sat down at the kitchen table with a big sigh, when Paddy entered.

"I believe congratulations are in order!" Martha hugged him once more.

"Oh yes. Me being a good catholic boy, I cannot continue to live in sin!"

Martha and Gabi burst out laughing in spite of the gloom that had settled a few moments ago. Then Gabi got serious.

"Paddy, he is getting off. And Emma wants to leave."

Paddy shook his head. "It is incredible, however in a way, I am not all that surprised. Unfortunately, guys like him have a way of getting themselves off the hook again and again. What is sad though is a mother who does not even give her daughter the benefit of the doubt. We need to sit Emma down, when she comes home. Running away is not the answer."

A few moments later Emma burst in. She had seen the car outside and knew they were back. She put her canvas down in the hall and peeped enquiringly into the kitchen. Martha smiled at her. "They are outside on the terrace."

Emma stepped outside. "Welcome back!!" She hugged them both.

"Maybe you should come along to the next speaking tour. I really missed you!" Gabi held her close. Paddy nodded. "Good idea – for a lot of reasons."

Emma looked at them in turn. "Martha has told you already?"

"Yes Darling. And there is no need for you to leave this place. We are here to protect you."

"He will be telling people his version. How can I face them?"

Paddy made her sit down on the spare chair. "You face them by knowing the truth. I know that at your age, it seems utterly important, how other people see you, what they think of you and so on. It is not. What matters really is, how you see yourself. You have endured his...unwanted attention long enough. You have proved to the world and yourself that you are made of better stuff. You are not the victim anymore. You asked for help, stood up to the bully and are in the process of building a good life for yourself. You have dealt with the past and are looking into the future. Allowing him to drive you away, would be allowing him power again. Do you want that?"

Emma remained silent for a few moments. She looked out over the beautiful bay. "I did not see it like that. I just felt fear and shame and pain..."

"Of course you did. That is the initial reaction to any kind of bad news...we allow our emotions to take control." Gabi took her hand. "Paddy has summed it all up very well. You have made such great progress in putting the nightmare behind you. He really cannot touch you anymore in any way, unless you let him."

"It might be a good idea to bite the bullet and go and see him and your mum one more time." Paddy said and looked at Gabi.

Emma stiffened in her chair. "I am not sure that I can do that."

"Not alone, of course. We will both be with you. And we will make him understand that you are off limits to him now and forever."

Gabi looked at her fiancé. She loved him even more in moments, when she was able to witness him stepping out of his comfort zone in order to do the right thing. Paddy could feel that she was looking at him. His eyes met hers, and all he could see was utter love. Until he had met this woman, he had never felt so unconditionally loved by someone who was not his blood family. She always made him feel special. He blushed. To distract from that, he changed the subject. "Emma, Gabi needs to show you something that will take your mind off these unpleasant affairs with your stepdad."

Gabi smiled and just put her hand with the gleaming engagement ring on the table.

"Oh my God!" Emma looked from one to the other. "That is so beautiful!!" She jumped up and hugged them both one after the other. "When will you have the big day?"

"We will have to think about that. And I need you to help me with the preparations." Gabi smiled at Emma again.

Emma now had tears in her eyes. "I am so happy for the both of you. And it is so romantic!! And I am so grateful for everything."

Paddy took a long sip of the now lukewarm tea and closed his eyes. He really had not known where the idea to get married again had come from; more and more though he realised that it was most likely one of the best ideas in his entire life. He had come such a long way from the man he had been, when he had allowed his need for the next drink to ruin his first marriage. Sometimes he took the time to reflect on the life he had made for himself. Many ups and downs, rough patches, shameful incidents, broken promises, broken hearts, pain, sickness, depression...and then the realisation that it was down to him to pick up the broken pieces and build a new life. And he had done. He had sobered up in every way, to the point where he was now an addiction counsellor himself. He had proved to his children that he was able to be the father that he had failed to be, when they were little. He had managed to build bridges to his ex-wife and gain her forgiveness. He had re-invented himself with a new and successful career. And then out of the blue he had met Gabi who from day one simply accepted him with all his flaws, issues of the past and never ever doubted him for a second. He had really tested her patience, because he had been so afraid to commit to a relationship again and possibly fail another good woman, when times got rough and he might not be able to stay away from alcohol. He had seen it happen many times with guys he met in the AA; the stress a relationship can bring, can really break down the determination of staying dry. Gabi though had not once become impatient with him and his reluctance; she always made sure to hang on to her love for him. And she used to say: "Paddy, you are worth the wait. I will give you all the time you need; maybe because I know, how this story will end!" And now they were going to get married. He opened his eyes again. Gabi was looking at him, Emma had gone.

"You were really deep in thought, gorgeous."

"Aye." He got up and pulled her out of her chair to kiss her and hold her tight. He still held her, when Martha called them for dinner.

16

The next day they decided to check out the progress on the cave access. Molly excitedly jumped around the area where work had started.

"What do you think? Can this be done without too many bigger problems?" Paddy shook hands with the guys who were working to ensure a secure entrance to the caves below.

"Well so far it does not look too bad, really. As you can see, we have put decent scaffolding down and secured the entrance. However, we still need to consider the further cave structure as well as the question: do you want this to be a temporary measurement or do you want safe permanent access to the caves below."

"Mhm now that is a good question. I don't think we need permanent access really. We just want to explore the root cause of banging noises we have heard in our house that definitely came from underneath."

The builders looked at each other. The foreman scratched his head after taking his hard hat off. "Ok leave it to us. We will see how far we get from this opening."

Paddy put his arm around Gabi, whistled for Molly, and they went on a longer walk. Emma had gone painting with her tutor again.

"We have not had any more banging recently. And Emblyn has not appeared again either. Do you think, we should just let it rest?" Gabi asked.

"I am surprised to even hear that question from you. Where is your sense of adventure?"

"Oh don't worry, that is still here alright. I just had a slightly strange sensation, while looking down into the cave just now."

Paddy stopped. "A foreboding?"

Gabi sighed. "I don't know what exactly. Just thinking: I hope we are not opening Pandora's box here!"

"Nah, I don't think so. I tell you what I expect: to find the skeleton of a girl there and that will be the end of it."

Gabi sighed and walked on. Something inside of her told her that they would encounter more than Paddy expected; however, that was just some kind of uneasy feeling, a premonition, nothing scientific, nothing that made sense even to her. So, she decided to let it all rest until they would be able to get into the caves from this end. Instead she allowed her thoughts to wander to Emma and the situation they had to deal with regarding her mum and step-dad.

"I think I shall give Emma's mum a call, when we get back from the walk."

"To alert them to our upcoming visit?" Paddy kicked a pebble on the ground; he was not a violent person at all; that man who called himself Emma's step-father though, he really made his stomach turn; he would love to get hold of the man in a dark corner and see to it that he could never again in his life use his cock for anything more than to have a piss.

Gabi could sense his tension. "Paddy, of course the man is scum. I just want to play by the rules and give them absolutely nothing they can use against Emma and us at any point."

Paddy swallowed – his anger, his disgust and his passionate desire to kick the man into shape. He silently nodded.

"Shall I offer them tomorrow for our visit? I just want it over and done with as soon as possible. It otherwise is a shadow over our heads that neither of us really needs."

"Yes, Gabi. You are right. Of course you are. I just really struggle with men like him."

"So do I; we are doing this for Emma. The Law unfortunately has taken his side. We have to accept that, as much as we think it wrong and despicable. All I really want is for him to understand that he may have fooled the court, he has not fooled us; we are now looking after Emma and helping her to gain back the confidence he tried to knock out of her. I want to get the message across that he has no more power over her and that he better stays away from her and us for good."

"It could well be an unpleasant encounter. After all, he will think by getting off he is now fancy free."

"Most likely. Paddy, we are counsellors...we need to just remember and use that to our advantage. And most of all, as hard as it will be, we need to mentally distance ourselves and not rise to any form of aggression, not verbally either."

Paddy looked at his fiancée and smiled. "Warning accepted, Miss!"

Over dinner that evening they discussed with Emma, how they expected the visit the following day to go. Emma was not entirely happy with the whole arrangement.

"He will be sitting there, sneering at me. And mum will just sit there and nod to everything he has to say."

"Darling, we do not need to talk about the past. It is done; unfortunately he managed to fool the Court. He now is not going to be a part of your life anymore. You have outgrown him already. We can just talk about the presence and future." Gabi put her hand on Emma's free arm.

Emma still looked uneasy. "Please do not believe his lies." Her eyes had filled up.

"Good God, there is no danger of that!" Paddy got up. He paced the dining room. "Given half the chance, I would tear his…"

"Paddy!! We did talk about this!" Gabi looked at him in a very calm, but firm way. "I need to rely on you remaining the centred and peaceful man that you are."

Paddy stopped, closed his eyes and took a deep breath. "Of course, Darling. I will be."

Martha got up to collect the dishes. "I am with you on this, Paddy. Men like him should be castrated – that is the least punishment I can think of."

Paddy hugged her. "Thanks Martha."

Gabi looked at Emma. She had gone very pale. "He is just such a good liar."

"Emma, I have seen all the bruises on you. Whatever he might want to say for himself, we are not going to believe him. All we want to do is explain the future boundaries to him. Now…what about your mum? Would you like to see more of your mum?"

Emma sighed. "She is my mum; she has taken his side, though. I don't even think that she would like to spend time with me."

"Ok, let's not speculate too much. We will just go there tomorrow after breakfast and see. Then we have done our bit."

17

With it being a lovely sunshiny day, they decided to walk to the house that used to be Emma's home. They did not talk much. When they arrived, Emma's mum opened the door. She looked pale and uneasy; however, there was a glimpse of gladness in her eyes to see that her daughter looked so well. She politely asked them to step inside and take a seat in the living room, where her husband was already seated. He did not get up to welcome either of them, just nodded and sneered at Emma.

Mrs Portland brought in a tray with mugs of tea and a small bowl of biscuits. She gestured for everyone to serve themselves.

"So, what is it that you want from me and my wife?" Mr Portland grabbed his mug and looked at Gabi.

"First of all, thank you for agreeing to see us today. We thought that it might be a good idea to briefly talk about future interactions between yourselves and Emma."

"I hope you have made sure not to leave the little slut alone with your man there – or you will..."

Paddy had risen. "Bloody hell, man; you really are a special specimen!"

Gabi grabbed his arm and with her eyes begged him to calm down and take a seat again. Emma's eyes had filled up. Her mother sat stiff and silent.

"We are not here to talk about the past, as we deem that absolutely pointless, Mr Portland." Gabi took a mug; her hands had gone ice cold, and she needed something to remind her that she had to remain as calm as possible. "We are here to let you know that Emma is living with us now for good. She has made that choice on her birthday. Given the circumstances of her leaving home, we think it might be advisable to limit future contact as much as possible."

"I am done with that slut anyhow. She hurt her mother enough. Good though that everyone knows the truth here."

Paddy tensed seriously. Gabi pressed her leg against his. "Mr Portland, it would be helpful, if you could abstain from the use of such language, when you are referring to your step-daughter. Like I said, we do not want to discuss what really happened within these walls. We just want you to understand that even though you managed to leave the court as a free man, there are many people who know the true story. Emma is off limits for you from now on. We do not want to take any legal steps at this point, however we will not hesitate to do so, if you ever try to approach her again anywhere. To make myself clear: stay away from Emma for good. As for you, Mrs Portland; if you want to make contact with your daughter we have no objections to that. It would have to be under Emma's terms though. Your daughter has suffered more than enough; she needs to and will be protected."

Mrs Portland looked from one side of the room to the other. She tried to meet her daughter's eyes, but Emma just looked to the floor.

Before his wife could even open her mouth, Mr Portland got up. "I don't know who you think you are coming into our house and telling us what to do. We do not take orders from anyone. You better shift yourselves – and for your information, I am a free man and can do as I please."

"Not where Emma is concerned. If you as much as make a step towards her at anytime, I will get a court order against you based on medical records. It is in everyone's interest to keep the future possible encounters as civil as can be. That is the reason we are here."

"I am not being threatened by the likes of you! Get out of my house!"

"Nothing here is yours! My dad bought this house...you are just a brute and a parasite!" Emma got up, stared at her mother and went outside.

Paddy was already standing and blocking the way for Mr Portland to go after his step-daughter. "Don't even think of it, man. You got off lucky once; next time there will be no luck for you. And if I ever have to see another tear out of that girl's eyes, because of you, trust me, you will..."

"Let's go, Paddy." Gabi put the mug down. She took Paddy's hand and gently pushed him towards the door. "Mrs Portland, thank you for the tea. I hope that in time you will be able to make peace with yourself and your daughter."

Outside Gabi took a few deep breaths. Emma sat on a wall opposite this house. Paddy just stood and tried to regain control. Gabi crossed the road and pulled Emma up. She took her in her arms. "Are you ok, love? I am sorry, we put you through this. He needed to see though that you are not alone and vulnerable anymore."

"He is evil scum! And my mum said nothing, nothing at all."

"She will in time. He controls her for now. The day will come, when she, too, sees the whole truth and throws him out."

"Remind me to not let you talk me into something like this again. Let us go for a long walk along the sea. I need plenty of fresh air now." Paddy started walking.

"I still think that we did the right thing in coming here and..."

"I can't believe how amazingly calm you were in there." Paddy had stopped and turned around.

"It was not easy. And I might get a headache later on, when all the tension leaves."

"I deeply admire you, Gabi. You were controlled, calm and yet firm. I do think that he has got the message."

"I think so, too. And now let's walk on and clear our heads. We have done our bit here. And we have a trip north to plan and …"

"…our wedding, mo gra!!" Paddy kissed Gabi and walked on with a smile.


"I think it is so romantic that you two are getting married!" Emma sat down with Gabi back in the house. Paddy had taken Molly for a walk.

"To be honest, I was really surprised, when Paddy proposed. Since we started dating, he has been going through what I used to call his insecurity loops; whenever I felt that we had turned a corner, and he actually was fully on board our relationship, he would withdraw for days or weeks; he used to say then that he was not ready, that he was simply not in the right place for commitment etc."

"Really? He seems so absolutely besotted with you."

"Well, for the first year I needed to muster a lot of patience. Luckily, I was really busy at work and with all my charity projects, and my writing. Also, I have always had a good circle of friends that kept me level headed. My own faith and following the teachings of the Secret helped me to let him go without giving up on him and us. He had so many issues inside of himself that we only managed to deal with by and by. He finally came back for good…I think what helped was the fact that I had decided to move down here. He realised that he needed to make some decisions."

"How did you know that he was the one that was worth waiting for…I mean, how did you know that he would come back and would stay?"

"Good question. I just felt that there was so much good about him, that he deserved my patience. Also, from the first date I knew that our story was going to be a long one."

"Hmm – well you were proved right."

"Indeed, I was. And I am so glad that I followed my gut instinct on this one; you see most people around me kept telling me to stop wasting my time and focus on myself…and just enjoy life with another man. However, I could not do that; Paddy had touched something inside of me that meant that from that point on I would be linked to him, no matter what. And believe you me, it was not all that easy to wait patiently for weeks and weeks and weeks. Granted I was very busy with my job, my counselling and charity work, my writing of course and my friends and Nick; still this yearning inside of me for finally being able to just be with Paddy, see him, feel him and listen to him and his good advice, that was growing stronger and stronger. I shall admit it now: I had come quite close to the edge of faith, when he finally showed up at my house and just took me in his arms."

"Seriously? He did that?"

Gabi chuckled, lost in the memories. "Yup! I was just getting ready to set off to a good friend's Jamaican birthday BBQ – she is a chef. Paddy had been invited, but then had disappeared to Ireland and been very non-committal for many weeks; I was to take my neighbours with me and had somewhat given up hope that he would come back, when the door bell went. Nick was out, I was only half dressed, threw my dressing robe on and dashed downstairs, half expecting my neighbours. When I opened the door and looked into his eyes, my heart really missed a beat, or a few ones. I just stared at him. He smiled and pushed me inside, closed the door, dropped his bag and just pulled me in his arms. He held me tight, whispered >I am so sorry!< and then kissed me."

Emma sighed. "and they lived happily ever after."

"Not quite, but close enough. Anyhow, shall we do a bit of wedding dress browsing?"

18

The next morning brought the workmen to the door.

"You are good to go down in the cave now. We have secured everything, and we have been down ourselves. It is all safe."

"Come on in and have a hot drink." Martha provided them with mugs of tea and coffee, while Paddy, Gabi and Emma got ready for the cave adventure. Appropriately clothed and with camera and pads plus a flask in a small rucksack, they finally left. The foreman gave Paddy some instructions. Then three excited explorers climbed down, while the workmen started packing up all their tools etc.

When their eyes had adjusted to the dim light in the cave and the torch beam, they started walking; Paddy was in the front, Emma took notes. Gabi felt a strange knot in her stomach. They had only had a few more visits from Emblyn since Paddy had employed the workmen to open the access to the caves. Somehow it was, as if she knew they were coming for her. They had been exploring for about half an hour, when they came to something that looked like a bigger opening. Gabi felt a strange pull towards the back of that big cavity, where they could hear water in the distance. "This must connect to the tunnels that lead up from the beach."

"Sounds like it. You are shivering, Gabi." Paddy quickly wrapped his arms round her.

"I think she is here." Gabi took the torch off Paddy, turned slightly and shone to a corner. Sure enough, there was a pile of something visible. Carefully they approached it.

"Oh my God!!" Emma stared at the pile. It looked like skeletons hugging. She froze and just kept staring.

"This looks like more than one person to me!" Gabi bent down. "Get the camera and take some pictures, Emma."

Emma just stood. Paddy smiled, took the backpack off her and got the camera out. He took a few good shots in the torch light. "We need to get these to the police as soon as possible."

Gabi nodded. "Forensic anthropology will have a field day!"

"You ok, Emma?" Gabi got back up and noticed Emma still staring.

"I think there is a baby amongst the other skeletons." Emma's eyes had filled up.

Gabi took her in her arms. "It is possible. However, it is nothing to do with you. Let us go back home and get the police out. Have you mapped our steps?"

Emma just nodded.

Paddy shone around this corner once more and then took the lead for their track back which seemed much shorter than the walk to the discovery site.

As they emerged back into daylight, the foreman greeted them. "I just wanted to hang around and make sure you got back ok. Did you find anything interesting?"

"Yes we did. A group of skeletons. I need you to seal the entrance for now. We will go and phone the police."

"Good God!" The foreman went back to his van and got what he needed to seal the entrance off, including a warning sign.

Paddy, Gabi and Emma rushed back home. It only took a few hours for the back of their house to be swarming with police and a forensic team.

They had to tell the tale of how and why they came to investigate the caves several times, independently and together. The police inspector pulled his eye brows up slightly amused, when he listened to their accounts of "Emblyn's appearances". He clearly had his own view on ghost stories. Still he had to accept the fact that it was an interesting coincidence – the apparitions, noises and finally finding of the skeletons. They indeed turned out to be three skeletons: a man, a woman and a baby. Dating and identifying the bones would take a while.

When they had the house back to themselves, they all gathered in the sitting room and talked about their discovery.

There was nothing there apart from the bones...I mean no fabric at all. Would that have completely disintegrated by now or does it mean they were naked?" Gabi tried to remember what she had learned about decomposing bodies and materials.

Not sure...good question actually. Most intriguingly – no one ever mentioned that Emblyn was pregnant." Paddy put his mug of tea down and ran his hand through his thinning hair.

Well some girls can hide that very well." Martha said.

All I can think is: they died together. Did they voluntarily die or were they killed?" Emma curled up on the sofa and looked into the distance.

Forensics will be able to answer that to a certain extent, I should think. I have to admit that really is not, what I expected to find." Gabi looked pensive.

That night Gabi woke to stare at Emblyn in the bedroom once again. Emblyn looked at her with watery eyes. She did not seem to be entirely satisfied with the fact that her remains had been brought out of the cave and were now examined.

We are working on it. I guess there is more to this..." Gabi stared at the apparition.

Emblyn stared back at her.

Paddy turned next to Gabi, and the ghost faded away. Gabi sighed, took a sip of her cold green tea and closed her eyes again. The realisation dawned on her that this was no longer just a romantic story about a girl who ran off with her boy-friend, but actually a murder mystery. A girl, her unborn baby and the man she loved had been slain in a cave and left to die, to rot. A triple murder that had been sort of covered up by the whole community with a blanket of stubborn silence. Someone knew – back then and still today. While Gabi snuggled up to her sleeping man, she decided that she would not rest until the full truth would be known and made public. She was a writer after all; this story begged to be told. And maybe there was even some kind of justice for Emblyn to be had along the way; otherwise her ghost need not remain restless and seeking contact with Gabi.

19

While having to wait for the results from the Forensic Anthropologist, Gabi had decided that it was worth having another word with old Jago. He probably had not parted with all he really knew. So after their weekly session in the youth club, Gabi and Paddy strolled to the harbour pub, where Paddy had first met Jago. And sure enough, the old man was inside. As he spotted Paddy, there was a flicker of unpleasant surprise in his eyes, before he forced himself to smile and wave at the couple. Paddy sat down next to him, while Gabi got the drinks in. As she sat down, Jago shifted uneasily.

"Jago, how have you been? Here, have a drink on us." Gabi smiled.

"Well, yes. I have been well. And I hope the same for you." He took the drink and placed it in front of himself trying to avoid eye contact.

"Are you not interested in what we might have found out about Emblyn??" Paddy took his soft drink and stared at the old man until he had to lift his eyes.

He coughed, cleared his throat and then looked at Gabi. "I hope she has not been troubling you too much."

"We found her, Jago. In the caves through an entrance that was blocked many years ago, behind our house, hidden in the fields."

Jago swallowed and looked from one to the other. "How can you be sure?"

"We found three skeletons in the cave, Jago. Emblyn, her man and her..."

"...unborn baby." Paddy finished the sentence for Gabi.

Jago nodded to himself. He took a big gulp from his glass. His eyes became watery. "I sort of expected something like that to happen one day."

"Come on Jago, you do know much more than you told us. This is now a triple murder, not a folklore anymore. You should speak up, man." Paddy's voice took on an unfamiliar edge. He really was annoyed with the old man now.

Gabi put her hand on Jago's. "We want her spirit to be able to rest in peace. She is still not gone...we need to find out, who did this."

Jago remained silent, breathing somewhat heavily. Then he emptied his glass and tried to get up. Paddy blocked his way. "Have a heart, man. Someone did something horrible here...and from where I stand, the whole town covered it up. Someone must know or at least suspect, what happened. The police are now involved. Everything will come out eventually. Do you want to be helpful or get the police talking to you in a less pleasant way?"

Gabi looked at Paddy. She loved his passion in trying to solve this mystery, however she sensed that pressure was not the right way to deal with someone like Jago. She got up as well. "Paddy, why don't you get us all another drink."

The Irishman looked at her and after a little hesitation got up and walked to the bar.

"Jago, I get it. You are protecting someone, aren't you?"

While a tear rolled down the old man's cheek, he looked at Gabi. And in a quiet voice he said: "I am sure that she did not mean to do this."

"Who, Jago?"

"I really cannot say. I cannot say after all this time. It is not going to make any difference."

"Jago, Emblyn and her unborn child did not deserve an end like this, did they now? Don't you think that the truth must be told? Emblyn still visits me and begs me to uncover the real story. She won't be resting in peace otherwise. Her bones may now be gone and can be buried, but her soul needs justice, needs someone to defend her."

Jago wiped his nose and eyes with his shirt sleeve, just as Paddy came back. Gabi looked at her fiancé and motioned him to sit down and listen.

"I really don't know all that much, and nothing for sure. There was only one person who Emblyn trusted."

"Yes...and who would that be?"

"Demelza, her sister."

"Can we talk to Demelza?"

"Demelza was sent to a nunnery after Emblyn disappeared. That is why there are no relatives here now. The parents are long dead."

"Do you happen to know, where exactly Demelza was sent...and maybe what she looked like."

"Demelza was a true Cornish beauty with flaming red hair down to her waist. She was at least a year younger than Emblyn. I was quite a bit in love with her..." Jago smiled to himself.

Paddy looked at Gabi with eye brows raised.

Gabi encouragingly squeezed Jago's arm.

"They were always together, the girls. Collecting herbs and stuff. They were sort of learning the trade from an old druid character."

"Why do you think that Demelza has anything to do with this triple murder?"

"No one else knew about Emblyn wanting to leave…and Demelza did not want to lose her sister."

"How do you know all this, Jago?"

Jago emptied his glass in one go. "I had started seeing Demelza. She told me."

"And you really did not try to find out, where Demelza had been sent to?"

"Of course I tried. They took her away at night. Her father did not come back for 3 days. And no matter how I tried, they would not talk to me."

Gabi took a deep breath. "Jago, this is all very sad. I really am sorry for all of you."

Jago smiled at her. "Twas a long time ago. There were other lassies…Demelza though for sure was the prettiest one I have ever seen. Your Emma looks a bit like her!"

Gabi thought a moment. "I have an idea. If I ask Emma, would you sit with her and describe Demelza from your memory, so that Emma can do a sketch that might help us find her or at least find out where her father took her all this time ago?"

"I think I could do that, yes."

"Good. Please come to the house tomorrow, Jago; let us try to piece all the parts together."

Gabi got up, kissed Jago on the cheek and turned to go.

"Thank you." Paddy put his hand on Jago's shoulder and followed Gabi.

Outside the pub, the couple looked at each other. "What a story!"

20

While Emma was doing her best to bring Demelza to life on her canvas with Jago's assistance, Paddy and Gabi exchanged thoughts with Martha at the big kitchen table.

"There is a chance that Demelza is still alive. After all, Jago is."

"Of course – we are only talking 50 years or so. The most difficult bit will be to find out, where her dad took her to. Since there are no other relatives about..." Paddy poured more coffee.

"Let us just do some internet research and find out how many places there are in Cornwall and Devon that would have been taking girls in; cloisters, nunneries – whatever they are called." Gabi got up to fetch her laptop.

Martha remained unusually silent and pensive.

"Are you hiding something?" Paddy pecked her cheek, while waiting for Gabi to return.

"No Paddy, of course not. I am just trying to remember, if I ever heard anything about Demelza. And I don't think so, which is strange, because I remember the stories about Emblyn disappearing."

"Well you can only have been a child, when it happened. And people in those days made sure not to touch certain subjects in front of children. Plus, the disappearance of a young girl is of course something of a romantic tragedy."

"Of course. Both sisters going though makes it even more tragic...the poor mother."

"Ay – and somehow I find it distasteful that the whole town sort of covered it all up."

"Maybe it was less of a cover up and more of a trying to give the poor parents some peace."

Paddy still looked critical, when Gabi returned. "Ok, let's see what the Internet will throw at us."

They looked at different websites, tried different angles, found some promising abbeys and cloisters, came across plenty that had been long shut down. Finally, Gabi closed her laptop with a big sigh.

"Enough for now. Let us go and see, how Emma is doing with the sketch." She got up and went to look at Emma's work.

"How are you getting..." Gabi did not finish. As she walked into the living room and saw the drawing on the easel, she was stunned. "Wow."

Emma turned and smiled at her. "Jago is pleased with the resemblance."

"Jago, you really did not exaggerate, when you said that Demelza was a beauty. And it is fair to say that there is a certain resemblance to our Emma here." Gabi hugged the girl. "Amazing work, Emma. She really looks alive!"

"Thank you. Jago's memory seems rather fresh on the lady."

Paddy entered with a bottle for Jago. "No wonder you fell for her, Jago. Who knows, maybe we will find her."

Jago grinned. "Not much good that would be – I am not quite the dashing young man anymore."

"True love sees beyond that." Gabi put her arms around Paddy and felt a deep happiness inside of her, and a gratitude for having this man in her life now that her own Spring and Summer had long gone.

The next day was spent with more internet research and packing, for their trip North was imminent. Gabi had booked them into a nice hotel in Manchester, so they could stop and have dinner and a good catch-up with Nick. After all, Gabi had not seen her son since her engagement to Paddy. And of course being the mother hen that she was, she really missed her son, when she did not see him for several months. Knowing you need to let your children go and actually doing it in your heart, are two completely different stories.

Suitcases and bags went into the car, Martha was hugged by everyone and Millie barked excitedly. The early morning sun added a special beauty to the scenery. Martha shushed the dog inside and waved the travellers off. When she could not see them anymore, she got herself another big mug of tea and went outside on the veranda that overlooked the bay. What a beautiful view it was. Martha smiled. Yes, she had had her fair share of pain and suffering, however now she was part of this amazing family and blessed with sharing their home. She loved Gabi and knew their friendship would last, no matter what. Life was good, really. When the mug was empty, she decided to give the house a proper cleaning while everyone was out and then take Millie for a long walk.

was mid-afternoon by the time Paddy parked the car at the Great John Street Hotel which was a former school turned boutique hotel offering trendy rooms and most importantly a rooftop terrace where they relaxed with a drink while waiting for Nick to join them after his lectures. When he finally showed up, he hugged his mum, shook Paddy's hand and stood staring at Emma.

Sit down and get a drink!" His mother smiled at him. He looked well. When he had sat down, she showed him her engagement ring.

Nick grinned at Paddy. "Nice one. Congratulations again. When will the big day be?"

"Not sure yet, mate. Aiming for the Spring, I believe. However, that is all up to the ladies." Paddy put his Soda water down. "Where are we going for food? I am somewhat hungry after the long drive."

"I thought we go to the "Cane and Grain" in the northern Quarter. Really cool place." Nick googled on his IPhone and showed them pictures.

"OK. Lets get a taxi and go." Paddy walked ahead, clearly ready for a bite to eat. Gabi took his hand, Emma followed with Nick. They exchanged a shy glance. "You look really gorgeous!" Nick's mouth let his thoughts out, before he could stop himself.

Emma blushed. "Thanks. I feel so much better as well."

21

Another leisurely day was spent in Manchester; Paddy met his own children, while Gabi caught up with some friends. Nick showed Emma around the campus and city centre. In the evening they all got back together for another nice dinner.

"I have been thinking, mum." Nick looked at his mum.

"Yes?" Gabi pushed her empty plate away and focused on her son.

"Would it be ok for Emma to stay here, while you two go on to Scotland? I would like to show her some more of the area...and she has expressed interest in looking into possibly studying Art up here."

Gabi smiled and pulled one of her brows up. "Well you are both adults, you do not need to ask permission, really. Of course. Emma, are you happy to stay under Nick's guidance?"

Emma bit her lower lip. "Yes I really want to see, what and if I could study here – I find the city very inspiring. And it will be nice to be around some other students."

"Great. I will just ask the receptionist to keep your room for a bit longer, and we will see you after the speaking events in Glasgow and Edinburgh."

"Of course both Glasgow and Edinburgh are very inspiring places, too." Paddy threw in.

"I am sure. However..." Emma was searching for the right words.

"...we would also like to get to know each other better." Nick finished for her.

"Right – well we have an early start tomorrow. Hence I suggest Gabi and I head back to the hotel now, while you two maybe develop your own schedule for the next days. See you at breakfast maybe?" Paddy rose.

"Sure." Emma nodded with a tender blush spreading across her face.

Gabi got up, too; she kissed Emma on the forehead and Nick on the cheek. "Good night you two! Look out for each other." Then she took Paddy's hand and walked out into the night with him. Outside the restaurant she giggled. "I wonder, if my son has actually fallen head over heels..."

"It happens, Gabi." Paddy pulled her close and kissed her.

While Paddy and Gabi enjoyed their time in Scotland, Nick spent all his free time showing Emma around all arty places in Manchester he could think of; they met his friends, went to talk to people in the Art Faculty about the chances for Emma to enrol and simply enjoyed each other's company.

Gabi had two successful events and simply loved being back in Scotland. Particularly Edinburgh had grown close to her heart – the special synchrony of old and new, modern and haunted, history and future, the aura of so many writers and artists that she claimed she could feel made Edinburgh her second home. They took a final stroll to the castle at night, sat on the wall and looked over the town. "I wonder what we will find, when we get back to Manchester…"

"Judging by the fact that we have not had many text messages from either of them, and definitely no disturbing ones, I guess we will find two young ones walking in a pink cloud." Paddy put his arm around Gabi.

"I guess so, too. And I will try to not stick my nose in and give any kind of advice."

"Haha that will be a first then, Gabi. You are a mother hen; you love them both. I can't wait to see you bite your tongue."

"Am I that bad?" Gabi leaned into his embrace.

"Worse. You want everyone you care for to be happy and fulfilled…just…life does not always allow that. Demons creep up…" Paddy sighed.

"What is haunting you?" Gabi sat back up and looked at the man next to her.

"Nothing…everything. I don't know. Don't worry. Let's walk back to the hotel and get some sleep."

"Paddy, you will tell me, if you feel troubled?!?"

"Gabi, I am fine. Why wouldn't I be?" He pulled her up and they went back to their hotel.


"Meet us at the hotel. We should be there in about half an hour." Gabi texted her son, as Paddy drove them to the City. He seemed restless.

When they walked into the lobby, Emma and Nick waited for them. They were sharing a hot chocolate and seemed very cosy in each other's company.

"How did it go?" Nick rose first to give his mum a hug.

"Very well indeed. And Edinburgh as usually was absolutely lovely. And you two?"

"Great…I mean we had a great time, too." Nick looked at Emma. "Amazing what Emma knows about Art."

"Also amazing what a gifted artist she is herself. Let us just take our suitcase upstairs and then have a decent chat." Gabi hugged Emma and crossed the lobby with Paddy who had remained quiet. They signed in and took the lift upstairs.

"And?"

"What?" Paddy put the suitcase down in their room.

"What do you think about the two love-birds"?

"They make a nice couple." Gabi just watched him quietly, as he got changed. She knew that some inner dragon had been awoken inside of Paddy; she just was not sure why and what that would mean. She chose to let him have some space.

"Darling, we will wait for you downstairs, ok." She quickly got changed herself and then left Paddy to himself. As she approached the lobby again, she could see Nick and Emma holding hands. It warmed her heart and made her forget her worries about her own fiancé.

"So you two, do you have any news?"

"We did all kinds of stuff, and Emma could get into Art classes for the Spring term. It is a real opportunity."

"I am impressed. And I am sure that you two have also used the time to get to know each other better? What did that lead to?" Gabi smiled.

"We...really like each other." Nick looked at Emma. She continued: "...a lot! We like each other a lot. Nick is amazing; and I even went to a Law class with him. It is all so fascinating here. And I hope that you are not mad at me for wanting to come up here."

"Darling, of course not! I think it is great that you can take Art lessons soon. And I also think that you two make a lovely couple. We should go for a celebratory meal. What would you like?"

"Not bothered. Shall we just walk around and see what we fancy?" Nick suggested. "How long will Paddy be?"

"Not sure; he seemed in a dark mood for some reason only known to himself. Lets go to the bar and have a drink, before we set off."

They went to the bar and ordered three drinks, Gin and tonic for the ladies and a lager for Nick. They chatted a good half hour; Gabi could almost touch the happiness and positive excitement the two young people oozed. She really was glad, and she felt a deep warmth inside of her.

"...hungry." Nick looked at his mother.

"Pardon?" Gabi had missed whatever he had said.

"I am getting hungry. Shall I go upstairs and get Paddy? He might have fallen asleep." Nick grinned.

"Ok. Tell him we are ready to set off now."

Nick went to the lift, and the two women looked at each other. Emma blushed. "I think I am in love with Nick. He is so amazing."

Gabi hugged her. "I am happy for you two. He could not have chosen a better girl. I am glad that you feel at ease with him. He is a lucky young man!"

Emma smiled. They finished their drinks. 5 minutes later Nick reappeared with a piece of paper in his hands. He looked worried. He caught his mum's attention and remained silent for a moment, clearly struggling to find the right words.

"Mum...Paddy....well here is a note from him."

Gabi took the paper and stared at her son. This scene seemed unreal. What on earth was going on with the man? She started to read the few sentences, and then read them again three times, before the meaning sank in:

> ➤ My wonderful Gabi, I am so, so sorry to have to do this. However, I need time and space to myself. I know, I have done this to you, to us before. It really has nothing, absolutely nothing to do with you. I adore you. Still...I need to go. I am still a restless spirit. I really thought that everything was going well and I had my demons under control. I am not sure what brought all this on, I just know that I need to be on my own. You deserve so much better. Forgive me, if you can – you will always remain the best woman that walked into my life. God bless, Paddy <

"Mum???" Nick put his arm around her shoulder. "What do you want me to do?"

Gabi swallowed hard. Then she looked up. "Nothing Nick. There is nothing that either of us can do. Paddy is a law to himself...When he needs to go, there is no stopping him." She wiped a tear off that was rolling down her face. As much as it pained her, somehow she had known that he was getting itchy feet. "Let us go for a walk and something to eat as planned."

"Are you sure?" Emma looked at her and took her hand.

"Yes Darling. No one has died – he might change his mind again...or I might." Gabi got up and let the way outside. She took a deep breath. She turned to see her son and Emma holding hands. Life was still good.

When she got back after dinner and walked into the room that now only occupied her own things and herself, she finally allowed herself to break down and cry. She had thought that Paddy was healed and committed – after all, he had proposed to her. She cried, poured herself a bath and sat down in the steaming water. When she got out, she knew that she could not allow herself to go down; she could not and did not want to go through this loop of non-commitment again. She towelled herself dry, generously applied lotion to her body and then went to bed. She checked her phone once – there was nothing from Paddy. She typed a brief message to him: "Good luck to you – it was beautiful, while it lasted." With images of their good times together she thanked the universe for having been granted this crazy but beautiful love affair. Then she fell asleep with a smile.

22

Martha was shocked, when she learned that Paddy would not be part of their setup anymore. She shook her head, put the kettle on, filled three mugs and took them through to the living room. Emma thanked her for hers and said something about going upstairs to unpack. She thought it was best to leave Gabi and Martha to talk.

Gabi took her mug, sat down and folded her legs underneath. She gave Martha a brave smile. "I would not be honest, if I said that these new developments did not hurt and that am not going to miss my mad and gorgeous Irishman; however, what I have always had as leading principle in my life is that people who want to leave should not be stopped. He tried – he just is not a man to settle down."

Martha looked at her. "He is an idiot, if you ask me. He is not going to find another woman who understands him and lets him be as much as you. And he adores you....I don' understand this at all."

"Martha, sometimes love is not enough. He needs to be free, so I am setting him free. I would be wrong to hold on to him or the thought of us. Emma and Nick are the future, and you and I will be fine, don't you think?"

Martha sighed. "I really like him as well. He was quite the charmer. Well, you never know..."

Gabi put her mug down. "No, I am not going to wait another time. Our story has ended Now it is time to accept that and move on. Thankfully I am busy and will be even more busy with the film project."

"Other mothers have handsome sons, too!" Martha got up and turned to go back to the kitchen. "I shall see to our dinner now."

Gabi smiled. Her heart would always keep a space for Paddy; she allowed a wave of gratitude to fill her for the times shared with him. He left good memories behind, they had been a great couple. Now it was time to shift the focus on herself again. Another re invention was on the cards.

The next morning Gabi woke up somewhat energised. She remembered now that she alone was the director of the movie of her own life. She was not responsible for Paddy's, no responsible anymore for her son's even. The relationship with Paddy had been a proper rollercoaster ride from the start; to be fair on the man, he had never said that life with him would be a gentle sail into the sunset. Realistically she was not put on this planet to be the saviour of lost souls; of course she would continue to support people – after all she was counsellor and life coach, too....and of course a writer. From now on her priority would be herself, her life and the goals she still wanted to achieve. She knew in her heart that Nick and Emma would be good together. They both had such lovely personalities and seemed great match. Maybe her time for romance was over, done and dealt with. Maybe she wou spend the next years of her life just with Martha and the dog, enjoying this beautiful house, the peace and calm of her life, gorgeous Cornwall and really focus on her writing. She had been blessed with the fortune of attracting the money that had enabled her to buy this house and never worry about bills anymore. She could live in abundance, particularly now with the film contract. She had the chance to travel and speak all over the world; her life was good, and she knew it. The time with Paddy had been elating, exciting and in many ways very happy. He was a good man, and she would deliberately only keep her good memories of him and their time together. Of course she missed his company, his love and tenderness, the way only he could make her laugh. However she was able to fully accept his decision without going to pieces, and she had no regrets. She smiled at herself wondering, if the universe would actually after all put a man in her path eventually who would be capable of seeing her and her well-being as his priority, who would be walking beside her and have no demons left to haunt him. Demons? Ghosts! She still had to deal with Emblyn's story...time to get up and make footprints in the sand of life!

After breakfast, Gabi addressed her thoughts by seeking Martha's advice. "I thought that we need to get to the bottom of what really happened in that cave all this time ago. So we really need to try and find Emblyn's sister. We narrowed our search down to two or three possible places where she could have been taken by her father back then. Do you think that a drive out to these and asking some questions would be a good idea?"

"If you want to get to the bottom of this story and the triple murder, then absolutely yes. It is the only thread we really have." Martha decided to put the kettle on again; after all any kind of planning is better done with a cuppa.

"And do you also think, that...."

"...that it might be a good idea to bring Jago along? Yes definitely."

Gabi laughed. "So you can read my mind now as well?"

"Of course not; however it simply makes sense. He seems to remember that Demelza very well...and even though she, too, will have aged, he will be able to recognise her. You know..." Martha grinned..."through the eyes of love."

"Wicked!" Gabi got up to get her laptop. Emma radiated her still relatively new feelings of love and happiness and looked from one woman to the other. "Miss Marple is nothing against you two!!"

"Too right, sweetheart. Would you like to come along? You might get some inspiration for new paintings. Some parts of the north Devon coast line are really dramatic."

"Yes we could make it a proper outing – all of us tracing secrets back to the past and then turning them into novels and paintings."

"Good, we are all taking the time out then and going on an adventure. I will go to the harbour and see, if I find Jago. Maybe you two could meanwhile organise what we need to take, if we all leave the house. Let us plan the route first though."

Gabi found Jago in the pub as expected. She bought a round and sat down with him. He looked at her enquiringly, wondering where Paddy was. Gabi understood his silent question. "We have parted ways; at least for now. Paddy is a restless spirit, a wonderful man, but hard to tie down."

Jago nodded. "You are a fine, strong woman. You will be ok, with or without him."

Gabi smiled. "Thank you, Jago. That is good to hear. I agree that I will be just fine, as long as I keep busy. And that is why I am here. I have decided to attempt to track down Demelza. And I wondered, if you want to come along on the adventure with us girls?"

Jago looked at her and sighed deeply. "Oh I don't know. I am really happy to help you, but..." he emptied his glass and remained silent.

"Is it that you do not want to open old wounds? Are you worried that you might still have emotions for Demelza. Or are you afraid of what we might find?" Gabi leaned back in her chair.

Jago just grunted. His eyes became somewhat watery and he seemed lost in memories. Gabi decided not to push him any further. After all, they had the painting, had a name and rough age. She gave Jago a quick hug. "I understand, Jago. Sometimes it is better to keep the memories from long ago, rather than disturb them with new reality. We will be setting off around 10:00 tomorrow morning from the house – in case you change your mind. You are welcome to come along; however we can always fill you in on the findings, when we are back. We have narrowed it all down to three places, the most promising being "The Poor Clares" in North Devon. I think we will drive there first. Look after yourself!" Gabi left and paid the barman for another pint for Jago.

23

They set off with a full car – Gabi was driving, Emma sat next to her, Martha in the back and Millie in her travel cage in the boot. They had overnight bags with them, a basket with food and a cool box with drinks. Of course Emma's sketch of Demelza was with them, too. They had decided to take the picturesque coastal path and visit the Monastery of Poor Clares first. Somehow that felt like the most likely place – and Gabi had definitely learned to follow her gut instincts. Jago had not showed up; and Gabi respected that. After all she could brief him on their return.

Half way to Lynton in North Devon they decided to have a little break, take the scenery in and have a brew and sandwich. Gabi was just enjoying her second cuppa, when her mobile phone hummed. She answered.

"Yes? Oh, ok. " Gabi was listening for a while without any interruption. Finally she took a deep breath and opened her mouth. "I am very grateful to you for letting me know. We are just out on a little trip for a few days. When we are back home, I will be in touch and come and see you. For now it helps my understanding of the whole situation that we can definitely rule out natural death. Thanks again for keeping me in the loop." Gabi put her mobile down and turned to the two women next to her.

"That was the Forensic anthropologist in Exeter. They have finished their examination of the skeletons for now, are still waiting for some results." She paused.

"Yes??" Martha and Emma asked at the same time.

"Well there are two main points so far. The position of the baby and the bone age suggests that the baby was not born yet. There are no weaponry marks on any bones, including the skull. However they are waiting for some test results to confirm their thinking that the two adult skeletons were poisoned – now that could of course have been a suicide pact, or murder. They are looking for traces of Ricin which is a natural poison found in castor beans that can be traced in bones many years after consumption. They are also checking for mercury, lead and arsenic."

"Wow. My bet is on murder rather than suicide." Emma looked into the horizon.

Martha sighed. "I remember Jago mentioning that both girls had learned some natural medicine from an old relative. We need to ask him again...it could well be that they were the descendants and thus students of an old Sacred woman. Druids and witches are still very much a part of the pagan society in these parts of the United Kingdom."

Gabi nodded. "Yes, he did mention that. Well lets finish here and continue our journey. Who knows what we will learn, if we are lucky enough to find Demelza and get her to talk to us."

Emma took a few pictures with her phone to support a painting she wanted to do of the indeed dramatic North Devonshire coast line with its cliffs and crashing sea-waves. Then they set off. As they finally approached Lynton on the Exmoor Coast, Gabi felt a strange anticipation grow inside of her. Somehow she knew that they had indeed chosen the right location and would get answers here in order to help Emblyn's soul rest. They followed the signs for "The Poor Clares"; they knew from their internet search that this was a Franciscan Monastery founded about 800 years ago by St Clare of Assisi under the guidance of St Francis. The nuns led a quiet and poor life based on the approach from a woman for women. They parked up, and got out of the car to stretch and take Millie for a quick walk before walking to the actual Monastery. The location was breathtakingly beautiful, and there was peace and calmness tangible in the air.

"Do you want to go ahead on your own first to test the water or shall we all go?" Martha put the dog back in the boot.

"I think that we can very well go together, and also take Emma's sketch with us. See how it goes – and then find a place to stay the night."

They walked to the main gate and were immediately welcomed by a friendly nun who asked them, if they had come to the monastery for help or to spend some time in the retreat.

Gabi looked thoughtful. "Maybe a bit of both, sister. Mainly though we are here in the hope to find a woman from Cornwall who came here as a young girl and would be in her late sixties or seventies now. Her worldly name used to be Demelza…"

The nun whose name was Sister Magdalene seemed to think for a few moments. Then she nodded silently. "Please take a seat and serve yourselves with a drink, while I go and talk to Mother Superior."

Martha handed a drink to the other two and sat down. "I find the atmosphere very calm and comforting here."

Emma nodded. "I feel that we will get some answers here."

Gabi made some mental notes about what she wanted to say and moreover ask, given the chance.

Not long after Sister Magdalene had left, an older woman in the habit of a Mother Superior opened the door and smiled at them.

"Good afternoon, ladies. God be with you. I believe that you are looking for Demelza?"

"Good afternoon, Mother Superior." Gabi bowed towards the other woman. "Thank you for seeing us. Yes we are looking for Demelza from St Ives."

"May I ask what leads you here looking for her."

Gabi took a deep breath and then gave a concise summary of recent events and the bits that Jago had told them about the two sisters Emblyn and Demelza. "So really we just want to understand what really happened back then, and thus give the soul of Emblyn closure. Demelza might be able to help. We also have a sketch of the way she must have looked as a young girl." She nodded to Emma who handed the drawing to Mother Superior.

Mother Superior took it and looked at it for a while. She smiled. "Beautiful," was all she said before handing the portrait back. "Have you ladies got a place to spend the night?"

"Not yet. We have a dog with us and were hoping to find a B&B somewhere in Lynton."

"Please feel free to be our guests. We have a self-catering flat that you are welcome to use. While you set yourselves up there, I will talk to...someone who might be able to help. You are welcome to join our evening meal and prayers."

Gabi looked at the others who seemed quite happy with the suggestion. "Thank you very much, that is so kind of you."

"You are more than welcome. One of the sisters will come and show you the way and explain the location to you. I shall see you after my own little conversation." Mother Superior got up, smiled to them all and left, soon afterwards replaced by a young nun introducing herself as Sister Maria.

They put their things in the flat, saw to Millie and then sat down for a little de-brief.

"They are more than welcoming here," said Martha.

"Indeed. I do have a good feeling about this." Gabi stroked Millie.

"Shall we all attend the Evening prayer at 18:00h then?" Emma took a cardigan.

"Yes, lets go." They left Millie and went to the chapel. They sat down at the back. Some heads turned with a smile and then looked back to the front. One older nun kept looking at them with interest. She had a stunningly beautiful face. She locked eyes with Gabi and then nodded briefly, turning back.

After the prayer Mother Superior came to find them. "Blessed be you; I have talked to the lady in question for you. She will come and find you after her evening duties tonight in the flat. She will answer your questions. Please know that she is a very kind and loving woman. Her name is Sister Elisabetha. "

"Thank you so much." Gabi bowed to the Mother Superior and then followed the other two to their flat.

24

They were just relaxing with another cup of tea after their dinner of cold meats, cheese and pickles with rustic home-made bread, when there was a knock on the door. Millie barked.

"Shshhh!" Martha sent her to one of the bedrooms. Gabi opened. As expected she was looking at the beautiful face of the nun she had noticed earlier.

"Please do come in. Can we offer you something?"

"No thank you, I am fine. I am...I was Demelza in a previous life. Mother Superior told me that you have come all this way in order to help my sister's soul rest in peace."

Gabi nodded and pointed to the sister to sit down. Sister Elisabetha took the chair and then looked with great interest at Emma, who blushed.

After a brief introduction Gabi told Demelza about the recent happenings in their home and the finding of the skeletons. Demelza kept nodding, however remained silent. Only when Gabi had finished, did the nun take a deep breath. Her eyes had filled with tears brought on by the painful memory of what had happened all those years ago, and her part in it. She took a deep breath and then started her account of what happened in those caves all those years ago.

"I have tried to bury the tragic story of my sister deep inside of me; coming here even though it was not through my decision initially turned out to be the saving of me and my soul. I will tell you Emblyn's tale only because from what you have told me, she needs closure. Also I feel that I can trust you." She smiled briefly. "And dear Jago, still thinking of me. Apart from the Lord Jesus Jago really was my only love. Please tell him that."

" I think you could do with a nice cup of tea now, " Martha squeezed the nun's hand and got up to put the kettle on. Emma got the mugs ready. Settled with a fresh cuppa, they all looked at Sister Elisabetha expectantly. She took a sip of the steaming brew and started.

"Emblyn really loved Jocelyn. He was a stranger that one day just appeared out of nowhere. He met my sister during one of her daily walks along the coast; she really was a part of Cornwall with heart and soul. Jocelyn came from London, somewhere in London. He was a young lawyer.

When they met, Jocelyn was smitten with my sister...all that she was: a wild woman, natural beauty, caring, loving and so in one with the sea. She loved him from the moment they first laid eyes on each other. He seemed to reciprocate her feelings. After the initial trip to Cornwall he kept coming back; of course he loved the county, but most of all he was irresistibly attracted to Emblyn. To him she was so unlike any woman he had ever known in the City. By and by he got her to trust him, to believe him...and to awaken a raw and wild passion in her. Finally they started making love.

Both Emblyn and I were from an early age taught by our grandmother to collect, prepare and use natural medicine, herbs, flowers, barks and roots...I think that is a reason why the people in the village were always a bit weary about us...including our father. Female empowerment was not really his thing." Sister Elisabetha chuckled. "Probably a key reason why he wanted me gone and placed in the care of others." She took a few more sips of her tea and then continued.

"The inevitable happened: Emblyn fell pregnant. We talked about the options – like I said...we had learned about the various uses of various herbs etc. However my sister did not want an abortion. She believed in Jocelyn and his love for her. She was sure that he would do the honourable thing and marry her – the new life inside of her made her torn between her wild instincts and society's norms and expectations. She wanted to do right by her child which of course had been conceived in love.

When Jocelyn next came to see her, everything somewhat changed. He noticed that her figure was somewhat rounder, her breasts fuller, as he undressed her. She enjoyed the love-making again and then told him that she was with child. His reaction was not quite what she had expected. He abruptly got up and paced up and down like a caged tiger. Yes he loved being with her, he loved her passion – but he never had had the intention to marry her. She was his secret escape from the stressful life in the City. He did not want to give her up, she aroused him in unknown ways. So Jocelyn got trapped in his own web of lies.

As we learned by and by – because he did keep coming back – he was already engaged to a woman of wealth and connections in the City, a woman closer to his own age. Emblyn was only 16 when they met. By the time she understood that he would really never marry her and do right by their child, her heart died; she stopped being the life embracing, passionate girl that was my sister. Instead she asked for my help." The more she talked, the more Sister Elisabetha became Demelza again. She now had tears in her eyes.

"I don't know, if I did right or wrong. Definitely I did not understand the full extent of her decision that day in the late summer. She was my sister, I loved her with all my heart and it hurt me to see her broken. No one had actually noticed her pregnancy. She was one of those who don't show until very late. So of course by the time she made her fateful decision, the time for an abortion had long gone. We went to collect castor beans and to extract the Ricin in them. As far as I understood, she wanted to punish him for having led her on. And I thought he deserved punishment for ruining her life and not being willing to take the responsibility. So I helped her. I should have been suspicious about the amount of Ricin we collected, but I believed her, when she told me that she just wanted to be on the safe side."

Demelza's eyes now were sparkling with tears. The memory upset her deeply. "The last time I saw my beautiful and kind sister she was dressed in her best clothes with a lovely new shawl over her shoulders. She looked radiant, as pregnant women often do. She hugged me and made me swear to not tell anyone anything about Jocelyn and the baby. She said that when I saw her again, all would be fixed…" Demelza took a tissue that Gabi had offered. Martha refilled the kettle. Emma dried her own tears. Finally Demelza picked up the thread again.

"So while I thought that my sister was going to poison the man that had ruined her life and come back to me, she went to see him at the cave one last time. Like I said: he could not stay away from her and Cornwall. The next part is obviously now not based on conversations with my sister; it is what I think happened. They went into the caves to make love. This time though she must have taken him deeper than ever before. After making love she gave him the poison in a prepared drink, and then drank it herself, too. They might have become a bit drowsy, cuddled up and died in each other's arms. No one ever found them, no one ever heard from them again. No one from London came to look for Jocelyn, so he really must have kept the affair with my sister and everything about it a secret. Until you coming here and telling me about the three skeletons you found, I did not really know the end of the story of my sister and the love of her life. A part of me had always hoped that he had come one last time in order to take her with him and that they had eloped and were happy somewhere…obviously that was foolish. Leopards don't change their spots, they say…My parents were very disturbed by Emblyn not coming home that day, nor the next. I was questioned again and again; however I have kept my promise. So everyone thought that she must have gone for her usual walk, lost her footing and been swept out to sea. Then rumours started, because of course some people had seen Jocelyn, when he had come to stay, and some had seen Jocelyn and Emblyn together, kissing. My father was besides himself with rage and shame, calling Emblyn a whore who had probably now run off with that stranger…" Demelza took a deep sigh. "And when he saw me with Jago, he snapped. He swore that not another of his daughters would end up like that. With my mother sobbing her heart out, he threw a few of my clothes in a suitcase and set off with me in the middle of the night. And that is how I came to Lynton and after a period of adjustment under the kind guidance of the nuns around me finally found my peace with myself and happily became a Sister."

Demelza finished her cup of tea; everyone was silent, lost in their own thoughts. Martha looked at Demelza. "It cant have been easy for you back then. And now we have come and sort of taken away your comforting thoughts that your sister had after all simply run away with the man of her heart after convincing him to do the right thing."

"Yes." Gabi nodded. "I am sorry to have disturbed your peace like that. I feel bad about it…however please rest assured that I have not come here for selfish reasons; your sister kept begging me to help her. And I just really did not know where else to look for a conclusion now and who else to turn to."

"It is fine." Demelza spoke softly. "We all need closure, I think. And realistically it was only the foolish girl in me that held on to the false hope; deep inside I think I always knew that she would not just kill him, but wanted to die with him. He had made it impossible for her to carry on living in our community, our family, with not only having entered an affair with a stranger, but worse about to give birth to a child out of wedlock. And realising that while she loved him with all her heart, he was really just addicted to the sexual side of their relationship and would always have denied my sister...I think she saw no other way; and unfortunately back then I did not have the maturity and knowledge to give her comfort or a way out of her desperation. Life can be very challenging..." Demelza closed her eyes and seemed to push another unwelcome memory away. She looked at Emma, pondering something. But then she shook her head. "It is late, I will have to go now. I trust for you not to use what I have told you in any way that might dishonour my sister even now. Of course I do understand that you might need to tell the investigating police officers...they do not need to look for a serial killer...my sister poisoned her lover and then herself and her unborn child." With a big sigh Demelza got up and embraced each of the women. She held Emma a little longer, then blessed everyone and left.

25

"It is a sad story," Martha said again in the car next morning. They had said their good-byes and Gabi thanked Sister Elisabetha once more for her trust and for telling them the story of her sister. When she hugged the nun, she could feel for a moment that she wanted to say something more. Gabi looked at her; Demelza emerged for a few moments in the nun's eyes. Gabi looked at her again and then just fished one of her business cards with all her contact details out of her handbag. "Please let me leave you my details. In case you want to talk about anything else or remember something more that you might want me to pass on to either the police investigators, Jago or whoever...really I am always there for you, Demelza!" The nun had smiled, nodded and taken the little card.

"It sure is," said Emma. "And I do think that Demelza felt guilty deep inside for all those years. She seemed less tense this morning."

"I am a great believer in unburdening your soul to someone who is willing to listen and not judge and not use what they hear against you." Gabi drove along the picturesque coast line. "She still is a beautiful woman. I am sure that Jago would love to see her."

Martha chuckled. "Without a doubt. Now...what will you do with the story that Demelza gave you? Will you let the police know? Will you use it for a book?"

Gabi thought for a moment. "Since it is not incriminating Demelza at all, I shall let the investigating officer know what she told us. I think changing a few details, the story will make a cracking novel. I will also invite Jago round and tell him that Demelza felt as deeply for him as he for her. After all, we all like to know that someone is thinking of us with love in their heart..."

Emma and Martha exchanged a glance. Gabi became silent for a while, letting her thoughts reach out to Paddy. She had not heard from him at all, however he still owned that place in her heart. Thankfully she was going to be busy until Christmas. Scandinavia next week, then the USA and after her return the big family Christmas here. She smiled and reminded herself that there was so much to be grateful for in her life, and that Paddy had definitely added a lot of joy and beauty to her life, while he shared it. He was a very special man.

As they got home, Martha and Emma unpacked, Millie excitedly raced around the house and garden and Gabi looked through the post. Then she put her notes in the office and got her mobile out of the handbag. There was a message...from Paddy. She smiled and sat down on her office chair to read in peace.

"My dear Gabi, I thought of you so much today, I just had to drop a note. Fair enough, if you do not reply – I don't really deserve to hear from you ever again. I hope you and everyone else there is well and that the young folk are still happy together. Don't think I don't miss you...us...I do. Just that emotionally and mentally I am not in a good place at the moment...I am just not the man that you deserve; I am not reliable. You really are better off without me. I guess I shall never find out what happened to Emblyn the ghost…Look after yourself xxx"

Gabi took a deep breath and put the phone down. She had to think before replying to Paddy. She went to help the other two get the stuff sorted that they had taken on their trip. Martha decided to defrost a stew and already filled mugs with tea. Emma looked at Gabi.

"Are you ok? You look, as if you had some bad news?!?"

"News? Yes, not bad though – just unexpected."

"Paddy?" Martha put the mugs down on the kitchen table.

Gabi nodded and summed the text up. Emma smiled at Gabi. "He still loves you, I knew that."

"Ay, so he does." Said Martha. "Just sometimes love is not enough. His gremlins are taking hold of him again – I hope he does not fall off the wagon."

Gabi looked thoughtful. "I don't think he will. He has developed many coping strategies. He is very good with all his AA work…I think that he really is torn between wanting to commit and his own Angst around it all."

"You are not his carer, though!" Martha took hold of one of Gabi's hands. "He must be able to sort himself out, realise his frailties, deal with them. And only then will he be able to understand where his priorities should be."

"While I agree with that, Martha, I also think that if you truly love someone, you must be able to take your ego back and not blame the other one, but show patience and understanding for and with their struggles. Maybe it is good to step back and let them grow themselves…however they must know that the door back will always be open for them."

"Gabi, whatever you do, do not put your life on hold for him again." Martha got up to check on the defrosting stew.

"No that is not what I mean."

Emma was unsure about what to think and say. For the first time in her life, she felt wonderful, warm, wanted and safe with a man and in addition to that with his family. She was looking forward to seeing Nick again and not just talking to him over the phone. How would she feel in Gabi's shoes?? "I don't think it is easy to allow someone that kind of space…"

"No, it is not." Gabi smiled at her. "Still when you have come to understand another person and their dark side to a degree, you will become capable of not taking everything the other one does personal; and that is very liberating. Also at all times in life you must make sure to do what is the best for yourself...holding on, letting go...giving space...all along you must keep doing the things you love and giving your love to the world around you. And you must have faith and trust and feel gratitude for all the good in your life." She now knew how best to respond to Paddy. So while everyone went to their room for a shower and change into comfy clothes, she took her mobile along and replied to Paddy that he had never let her down, as he had always been honest about his demons; she also wrote that she still had faith in him and believed that they as a unit would be worth the faith and the time.

The next morning Gabi phoned the police and told them briefly about what they had found out. As expected they asked her to come to the station and sign a statement. On her return she stopped at the harbour and looked for Jago. The moment he laid eyes on her, he knew.

"You found her." He looked up and met her eyes.

"Yes Jago, we did. You will be pleased to hear that she is well and still as beautiful as in your memory. Also she is a very kind and gentle woman."

Jago nodded. "Oh ay, she was a stunner back then. Was she able to help you?"

"Yes." Gabi summed up what Demelza had told them.

"I knew she would not have intended anything bad to happen to her sister. Emblyn had strong mind of her own, though..."

"Indeed. The whole story is such a tragedy." Gabi softly touched Jago's rough fisherman' hand. "She also told me to tell you that you still are and always will be the love of her life."

Jago took a deep breath. With wet eyes he smiled. "Thank you, Gabi."

"Thank you Jago. Without you, we could not have helped Emblyn's spirit to find peace."

"Well all this has certainly brought back a lot of memories. And thoughts of what could have been."

"Jago, it is never too late to realise your dreams. If at any point you would like me to take you to see Demelza, just say the word. You never know what could happen..."

"Oh no, I could not possibly disturb her peace. She is in a good place, in every way. certainly have nothing to offer her."

"Jago, the decision is yours of course. I have only made the offer. After all she did give me pretty strong message for you."

Jago looked at Gabi. He swallowed hard and then nodded quietly. Gabi said her good-bye and went home. Before entering the house she quickly checked her mobile phone.

A short reply from Paddy greeted her: "You are an amazing woman...I wish I was a better man! Look after yourself, Paddy xxx"

26

Gabi was just saying good-bye to Viv after their safe return from Scandinavia, when her mobile phone rang. She did not recognise the number, so decided to take the call.

"Yes, this is Gabi. How can I help?"

"Hi....this is Sister Elisabetha...Demelza. I would like to talk to you, please. I have done a lot of thinking recently, well after your visit. And I need to know more about Emma."

"Emma? Mhm – do you want to talk now or do you prefer me to come and see you again for a face to face conversation?"

"I do not want to incommode you; however it would be preferable to talk in person."

"I have just landed in London from a trip to Scandinavia. So I could drive home via Lynton. I guess I could be with you late this afternoon. Then we can talk, and I set off home tomorrow morning. Would that be ok for you?"

"That is wonderful. Thank you, Gabi. I shall have a room ready for you. Drive safe."

While setting off for Devon, Gabi phoned home hands free. She let Martha know, that she would stop over at The Poor Clares and explained why.

"Emma? I did notice her repeatedly looking at Emma, when we were there. Interesting. I look forward to what you will have to tell us, when you come home tomorrow."


Gabi and Demelza had hardly sat down, when Demelza started the conversation with "I think that Emma may be my grand-daughter".

Gabi swallowed a few times. "What makes you think that?"

"Don't you think that she looks a lot like me?"

"Yes, we all thought that, when Emma did the portrait with Jago's help. But...have you ever had a child?"

Demelza looked down. She was trying to put her thoughts and emotions in order. Continuing to look down she started talking: "A little time after I arrived here and was still fighting in my head against the whole idea of me becoming a nun, a travelling monk appeared one day. He taught us all various things about faith, about our place in life; he was a very good listener and even greater storyteller. He was very kind. I liked him. He had beautiful green eyes that seemed to search your soul, when he talked to you...I had always been told how beautiful I was as a young girl. Still being more of a girl than a nun, I fell in love with him. I spent a lot of time with him...and I finally seduced him."

Gabi took her mug of tea and tried to suppress the urge to say something. She sipped some lukewarm tea and just looked at Demelza encouragingly.

"I am not proud of that. However it was beautiful to be with him...and we made love a few times. Then he left to move on, and I never heard from him again. But...soon after I realised that I was with child."

Gabi put her hand on Demelza's. "And in those days there was no other option for me...a young girl without family and without anyone to look after her...after my son was born, they took him off me. He was sent to the city to be adopted. He would be of the right age to be Emma's father...that is why I wanted to know more about Emma. When I saw her, I somehow felt strongly connected to her...but I could not really say more at that point."

Gabi nodded. She tried to put the facts in order in her own head about Emma's dad, her real dad; the few facts that she knew...from the gravestone and from conversations with Emma.

"The dates would fit perfectly. Do you think that Emma's mum would be prepared to talk to me about Emma's dad?"

"Mhm, that is a very difficult question. I have told you about the stepdad...he would definitely not encourage it; why don't I try to talk to her – maybe she can then write you a letter about her first husband. I do believe that theirs was a very happy marriage, and Emma has nothing but fond memories of her dad. He must have been a lovely man. I will talk to Emma and her mum for you...maybe you could come and spend a few days with us at some point; then you could also get to know Emma better."

"I have been thinking that myself. I shall talk to the Mother Superior about this possibility. Thank you, Gabi, you are most kind. Since Emblyn there seems to be a curse on the women of this family...or some kind of special challenge held for us. I am so grateful as well to know that Emma is with you and has recovered so well from the nightmare her stepfather put her through. No matter how far women have come with emancipation and all that, whether we admit it or not, men still hold such immense power over our well-being in many ways."

Gabi thought of Paddy and nodded. "It is true, Demelza. Even when we have learned that true happiness and salvation lies within us, we only are at our best with the right companion by our side..."

Demelza smiled. "In my case that would be The Lord. And still there is always a part of my heart that is longing for that special human touch...and I never ever forgot the beautiful little face of my baby boy. That is a unique yearning...somehow I am glad that Emma did what she did; she would never have been at peace with her baby created in such unsavoury circumstances. And now I am grateful to know that my boy grew up well, found happiness and left behind a beautiful and very gifted young girl."

Gabi and Demelza exchanged a look; both smiled in an understanding that only women can share without words. They hugged.

"I shall let you get some sleep now, you must be tired after all your travels." Demelza rose to leave. "I shall say good-bye before you set off tomorrow."

In the morning Gabi just finished her coffee, when Demelza came to see her again. "Good morning Gabi. I have spoken to the Mother Superior. She is happy for me to take some time out and visit you all, whenever it is convenient."

"Oh that is great, Demelza. I have one more trip coming up, to the USA. How about me then picking you up on the drive home from the airport?"

"That is a good plan, Gabi. I thank you so much for all you have done."

Gabi smiled. "Really it was your sister who alerted me; I just followed her trail. Now...would you like me to prepare Emma for your revelations? Or do you want me to leave that to you?"

Demelza took a deep breath. "It might be best, if you tell her what I told you. She trusts you – and she does not know me...yet, really."

Gabi nodded. "Ok. I will have a good conversation with Emma before your visit. I will let you know when exactly I will be back in the UK. Oh – what about Jago? Would you like me to tell him that you will be visiting? And do you think that you might like to see him again?"

"It might be a good thing, after all, he had never done anything wrong; and he was such a sweet boy – I have always remembered his tender touch with fondness." Demelza giggled.

The two women embraced each other once again, then Demelza waved Gabi off. When she reached home, two curious women expected Gabi ready with a big pot of tea.

27

Emma took the news very well; in fact she was positively thrilled to be part of this super interesting love story.

"So I am related to Emblyn."

"It looks like it."

"And that is probably why our personal ghost got so active, when Emma entered our lives!" Martha poured more tea. "What an extraordinary story."

"I wonder, if my mum knows anything about all that...I guess not."

"That really depends on how much your Dad knew himself. Are you in contact with your paternal grandparents...adoptive paternal grandparents I should say."

"No. I have not really seen them since dad died. I did hear arguments in the house about them still wanting to see me...of course HE put an end to it all. I am not even sure, if they are still alive..."

"We could find out about that, if you like. Anyhow one step after the other. You have enough to digest for one day!" Gabi hugged Emma.

"Can I tell Nick?"

"Of course my dear."

While Emma went upstairs to phone Nick in peace and break these thrilling news to him, Gabi and Martha prepared dinner.

"Paddy has been in touch." Gabi said while chopping vegetables.

"Has he now?" Martha looked at her.

"I get the impression that he misses us."

Martha nodded. "Of course he does. He is like a stray cat...but he does know where he could have a good home."

Gabi laughed. "A stray cat...really Martha."

"You know what I mean: he does not settle, but he would love to be able to. Paddy does love you in his own way. It just depends on what do you want out of this relationship with the crazy Irishman."

"Aye...if only I knew!" Gabi smiled.

The next day Gabi asked Emma, if she wanted to walk to the harbour with her and see, if they could see Jago. While they were walking Emma put her arm around Gabi.

"You are a very special woman. I wish that Paddy would come back. You deserve to be happy!"

"How sweet Emma. I am happy...I have such a great life and am blessed to be paid for what I love doing. Also I have Nick and you. I would be dishonest, if I said that I do not miss Paddy and the good times we had; however I have learned that you must let go of the bird that wants to fly away...otherwise it will be pretty in the cage you provide, but full of longing."

"Mhm, I have never seen it that way. That is a good image. And somehow I think that Paddy maybe just needed one more breakaway...I really don't think that this is the end of the story...and neither does Nick."

"You two lovebirds! We will see. Have you thought about trying to see your mum and talk to her about your dad, your real dad I mean? She might be able to confirm Demelza's story."

"I dunno. I am still weary of the step-father..."

"We could go and talk to her at work and then leave the decision to meet up at a convenient time to her...did you not say that she does a few hours in that lovely Italian place?"

"Yes...it used to be lunch to late afternoon. I guess we could try. I can't wait to see Jago's face, when we tell him that his Demelza will be visiting."

Gabi smiled at Emma. Since she had been able to leave the step-father and his abuse behind and had learned to feel loved and valued as a person, she really had blossomed. She was stunning looking young girl with a heart of gold. Nick was really lucky...Emma did resemble her grand-mother a lot, there was no doubting that. As they reached the pub that was Jago's favourite place, they ordered drinks at the bar and went to look for Jago. He was sitting quietly at a little table looking out over the sea.

"Mind if we join you?" Gabi put down a pint of local ale in front of him.

"Oh it is you. You all ok?" He smiled at them. "And thank you for the drink."

"We are very well, thanks. And we have some news for you." Gabi and Emma sat down. Jago stared at Emma. "You really look like Demelza. It is incredible."

Emma smiled. She put a hand on Jago's. "It is maybe not such a surprise after all. Demelza thinks that she is my grandmother."

Jago's eyes widened. "I thought she was a nun?!?"

Gabi grinned. "Indeed she is. However she gave in to temptation at some point – and there really is a big chance that Emma's dad was Demelza's son. But the story is not really for us to tell..."

Jago was still trying to digest this bit of information. Then he looked up. "She is going to visit, isn't she???" He seemed to be shaking. He took a big gulp of his ale.

Gabi could sense the turmoil of emotions raging inside the man. "I am going to the USA for 2 weeks on Monday. When I return I shall pick her up and bring her home with me. She will be our guest. She wants to get to know Emma properly....and she wants to see you again, Jago!"

"Oh no..." Jago put both hands through his hair. "I am a broken man. I can't face Demelza..."

"Nonsense Jago. You are a good man; you have had a rough life. Now you have 2 ½ weeks to think about how you want to meet Demelza, what you want to say and do, when you meet the love of your life again. And believe you me, Demelza will be just as nervous as you are. You two will have a lot to talk about!"

"No, I want her to remember the young dashing man that loved her more than anything in this world...not look at this wreck..."

"Well Jago, self-pity is not very becoming! You have plenty of time to sort yourself and to remember the man you were and the woman you loved." Gabi got up. "And don't forget that you are still my co-writer on my new novel!" She gave him a quick hug and then said good-bye with Emma following her.

Jago just stared into space, when they left. It had turned quite breezy, when they stepped outside. "Right my sweet: next stop is the Italian café bar!" Gabi lead the way.

As they entered the small café, they could not see Emma's mum. They found themselves a quiet table and sat down. A few minutes later, Mrs Porter stood next to them without yet realising who she was handing the lunch menus to. "Good afternoon, wha...Emma?"

"Hi mum. How are you?"

"What are you doing here?"

Emma remained silent. Gabi took over. "We are here for a spot of lunch...and because we wanted to have a word with you in private....without your husband interfering."

Mrs Porter opened her mouth, but then closed it again. A few moments later she said: "I finish here in an hour. I guess we could talk then for a bit. I will come back in 5 minutes to take your orders then..." she added a bit louder and went back to the reception area, where a couple with three children were just about to enter.

Emma and Gabi studied the menu. Both chose big Italian salads with crusty bread and large lattes. Emma's mum took the orders and served them quietly a little while later.

"Your mum looks stressed." Gabi said, when she had finished her salad.

"That's down to him. He never gives her a moment's peace."

Gabi nodded. That woman's life had probably turned much worse since her daughter left home. There was no other outlet for that man's rage now. If only she would be prepared to leave him and rebuild her life...

Mrs Porter came with the bill and told them that she would be waiting outside round the corner in five minutes. Gabi paid, and she and Emma left. As they turned round the corner Mrs Porter had tears in her eyes. "Emma, you look so beautiful, and so healthy." She tenderly stroked her daughter's face briefly.

"Where would you feel safe to go to and talk?" Gabi asked her. Clouds were gathering, and it started to look like rain was imminent. "Would you be ok with coming home with us and talking there? We live in the house on the top of the cliff."

"Yes. He won't be home for another three hours. I just need to make sure that I am back early enough to put the tea on."

They walked quickly back up to their home, Emma leading the way. She felt uncomfortable walking next to her mum. When she unlocked the door, Millie welcomed everyone. Martha did the same and then put the kettle on, while Gabi invited Emma's mum into the living room.

"Emma please take your mum's coat. Mrs Porter, please take a seat."

"What a beautiful, beautiful house...and the view is absolutely stunning."

"Thank you; I do feel very grateful to be here and be able to call this our home. Now we have some news to share, and we also would like to ask a few questions. However first of all let me thank you for agreeing to come with us and talk to us."

"You do know that I love you, Emma. And....I am so sorry that it all ended so badly at home..."

Emma swallowed hard a few times. She was torn between love for her mother, pity for the woman sitting there and also a good amount of sadness and disgust for the wife of her abuser who had at no point tried to listen and side with her daughter. She remained silent trying to work out how to best voice her thoughts in a way that would be balanced and honest, not sugar coated and not merciless either. She finally looked up and faced her mother with wet eyes.

28

With fresh tea the women sat and talked. Emma let go of her locked up pain. Her mother kept crying and nodding and just listening. She did not say much. Finally she got up after checking her watch. "I need to go home and make tea."

"Why on earth is he always more important than me?" Emma got up annoyed.

"He is my husband. And....it will only make him angry."

Gabi could see the growing anxiety in the woman. "When would be the best time for you to come back and talk to us about Emma's father...her real father?"

"I don't know...I suppose I could come tomorrow after work..."

"Ok. For now everyone has enough to digest, I think. I shall drive you home, so you don't lose more time. And we will be expecting you tomorrow early afternoon. Emma, please fetch your mum's coat."

Emma nodded and helped her mother in her coat. Then she spontaneously gave her a quick hug and dashed upstairs. Gabi lead the way to the car. Before reaching Emma's parental home Gabi glanced at the woman next to her and said: "Life is never just black and white, I know that. Emma is hurting; that does not mean that she does not still love you. As she gets older, she will understand you better, I am sure. Hopefully the two of you will be able to build bridges. Thank you for coming with us today."

Emma's mum sighed deeply and opened the car door to get out. "I hope that I am doing the right thing now."

As promised Emma's mum came back the next afternoon. She gratefully took the big mug of fresh tea and sat down with Emma and Gabi. Martha preferred to stay in the kitchen and listen to some music while browsing through the cooking books for some new inspiration.

"I loved your father very much. He was such a charmer, kind and gentle. He came as a visitor and fell in love with the area. He always said that the sea must have been calling him, as he felt so much more at home here than ever before in the city. When we met, it was love at first sight for both of us. I could not have been any happier than I was back then. We quickly got married and I quickly fell pregnant. And I have never seen a man more excited and elated than my Mike, when I told him that I was expecting..."

"Did you see much of Mike's parents?"

"They came down a few times, yes. They also seemed to like it here. And we visited them in their beautiful home in London."

"Did Mike ever say anything about being adopted?"

"Well, this is not something that was talked about much years ago. However he did know that he was adopted. He just did not seem to know or want to know much about his real parents...birth parents I should say."

Gabi and Emma nodded to each other. Emma finally asked: "Did you never want to know from nan who she had adopted him from?"

"Not really, no. I loved him and did not much care about his biological roots. Why are you asking anyhow?"

"Because we think that we have by chance come across Dad's birthmother. It is a long story...she is a nun now."

"Oh...and do you have any proof?"

"Not as in any paperwork, but this is her..." Emma showed her mother the painting she had done of Demelza.

"Oh my God, she is the spitting image of you."

"Exactly. Do you think that nan might have some more paperwork?? Do you think that it would be ok for me to contact her??"

"I really cannot answer that. I have not heard much from them since..."

"Since you chose to marry that bastard!! I wish you would leave him!!"

"It is not all that easy...and he is not all bad..."

Emma swallowed. "He raped me repeatedly and then tried to blame it all on me...I would call that rotten to the core. I had to have an abortion..." Emma started sobbing.

Her mother took in a few deep breaths. "I really did not know...I have no idea, how all this came to be...I was thinking of giving you a new dad, when I married him...he seemed to be so loving with you..."

"Too loving, Mrs Porter. You really need to protect yourself and think about what it is that you want for the future for yourself." Gabi interfered and put her hand on Emma to stop her from carrying on. "Would you be able to give Emma the address of your first parents in law?"

Emma's mum was in the process of getting up. "I will have a look, it must be written down somewhere. I need to leave now."

"Thank you for your help, Mrs Porter. And please remember that we are also here for you, if you choose to...change your circumstances."

Mrs Porter just nodded and left.

29

It was time for Gabi to pack again for Hollywood. She felt elated and at the same time somewhat deflated. Of course this was a marvellous success that she had achieved all on her own…some things however do not taste as sweet, if you cannot share them with someone special. Paddy should have been travelling with her and experiencing her incredible success with her; she still missed him at times. Of course she could function on her own and keep going on her own – she had done it before Paddy and would continue to do so. Still since he had left, it did feel at times as if a part of herself was missing. They had been such a perfect fit, inspiring each other and adding to each other's happiness. As she closed her suitcase ready for the morning, her I-phone pinged. She couldn't believe it…it was Paddy.

"Just thinking about you, as I seem to remember you must be getting ready for the USA trip today. I hope you all are well…would you believe me, if I said that I missed you?! X"

Gabi sat down on her bed. The cheek of the man!! She wanted to be annoyed with him, however she could feel her mouth slowly bending into a smile. It felt good to hear that he missed her, too. But…really that was not good enough. He said so from a safe distance, making sure he was safe from any relationship demands. What was it with men???

"Do they really only understand what they had, when it is too late?" Gabi took her glass of wine in front of the fireplace and looked at Martha, who was sitting in the other chair. Emma was in her room talking to Nick.

"Well, they certainly create the impression…a lot of them."

"I mean, we had it all, really. Plenty of quality time together, enough time on our own. A good life without any financial worries; both of us successful in their chosen occupations. We had so much to talk about, and everything else was just…perfect, too…"Gabi closed her eyes to visualise the last time they had made love. A smile hushed over her face.

Martha smiled at her. "I did not understand at all, why he left you – particularly after proposing to you. I mean…that was all his idea. They say that women are complicated…"

"Yes, that is a joke. I have never met a woman who would be going through these kind of changes or whatever you want to call that kind of behaviour, yet men…they seem to want everything, and when they have it, they can't handle it!"

Martha just nodded and observed the fire.

"Anyhow, we can focus on Christmas, when I come back. And of course I shall be in touch from California. I am still excited about the fact that my book is being made into a movie…to be on a movie set etc. Do keep an eye on our Emma; she was a bit shaken up today. I hope that all that Demelza has brought up will not do more harm than good for everyone."

"Gabi, everything will turn out right in the end. Do not worry about a thing!"

So she didn't. She flew to Los Angles in relatively high spirits and enjoyed the fuss that was made by the production company from picking her up from the airport in a limo to the chosen hotel etc. While enjoying a glass of champagne, she decided to reply to Paddy.

"Nice to hear from you and to read that you still think about me. I have just landed in LA – your memory was right. I am looking forward to the film project...however I would have preferred to share all this with you! Look after yourself x"

As expected, there was no reply from Paddy. He was very much a man who could not be ruled or tamed by the expectations of others or society in general. A bit like a wild mustang maybe. Gabi had a big smile on her face, when she entered the limousine that picked her up from the hotel and took her to the film studios where she was to meet the director, script writer and chosen leading actors and then spend time with the script writer and his team to adapt her novel to the screen. She felt like a superstar herself in this limo and with the service provided by the film studio...just shows you how much money is made in Hollywood the dream factory. She knew that she would probably have to accept some changes to her novel; she was just hoping that they were not intending to change key story lines or anything about her characters. She could accept criticism, however her books were like her babies, and she would have to think hard as to what and how much she as the author could go along with. After all she herself was usually disappointed with screen versions to the books she had read. She was interested though as to who they had picked for the lead roles. Just as they entered the studios she took a few deep breaths and decided to not be too stubborn, but open minded.

Pleasantly surprised by the people that she had met, she returned to her hotel room that afternoon with some suggested script ideas / changes to go through until the next morning. To be perfectly honest, she was finding it invigorating to see how much these people appreciated her novel and how much they had thought about what would work on screen and what would need to be adapted. She would meet the chosen leading characters for dinner at the hotel that night. So she decided to have a quick refreshing shower, make herself a pot of tea and go through the suggestions before getting ready for dinner. She was excited to see, if the chosen actors would come near to the characters she had in her head.

She was not disappointed. The actors were well chosen, and it filled Gabi with awe to meet people she so far had only seen on the big screen and discover, that most of them were down to earth. She smiled and did feel proud, when the lead female actress told her how impressed she had been with Gabi's novel and how she felt really honoured to help bring to life and give a face to such an interesting literary figure. All of a sudden it hit her, that she, too, had become famous – her work had indeed touched other people in many different ways. As an author you first write basically for yourself and for all the characters that live in your head and want to come out. As she had said in an interview a while ago

"You do not really invent stories; they already live inside of you. You are merely the tool that brings them out to be shared with others." Everyone wanted to talk to her and was very pleasant. She loved every minute of that dinner, and she looked forward to the work in the studio over the next fortnight. What an experience. For a few seconds she closed her eyes and said a silent prayer of gratitude to the universe. From the very first time that she had put pen to paper, she had somehow known that she really was born to be story teller. However she had not actually envisaged herself to be working with people from in front of and behind the big screen; it was amazing how her life seemed to get better and better. There was just one thing missing to complete her happiness...a certain Irishman. She smiled to herself, when a man handed her a glass of champagne and introduced himself.

"Hi, I am so pleased to meet you in person. My name is Raoul, and I am the main script writer on this project. Without trying to be cheesy, you have a beautiful smile...must be a special someone who causes this."

Gabi giggled. "Pleased to meet you Raoul, please take a seat. I just smiled in memory of my past."

"I loved your novel and am convinced that we can turn it into a huge success on the big screen. It really lends itself to be turned into a movie...the characters are so lively, so real...and the story is just beautiful."

"Thanks Raoul, that is praise indeed. What do you think are the main areas that need altering in order to make the novel more adaptable for the cinemas?"

"Not all that much, really. Your style is very descriptive as it is, and you have many great dialogues in the novel. I have re-read it and underlined a few things that we might have to work on a bit. I know that you are only here for a limited time, so when shall we get started tomorrow?"

Gabi felt an adrenalin rush. "Working breakfast somewhere suitable at 9:30 a.m.?"

Raoul nodded. "Yes that is great. I shall be back here at your hotel for that time. Now back to pleasure for tonight...do you dance?"

Gabi had not noticed that there was old film music playing in the background, and some people had taken to the dance floor. "If you lead well, I can dance ok!" She put her hand in Raoul's extended one and walked to the dance floor with him. He certainly knew how to move; it was a pleasure dancing with him. Hence it was much later than planned that Gabi fell into her bed for a well deserved round of sleep. She did not hear the messages arriving on her phone until the alarm woke her up to remind her to get ready for business.

The first message was from Raoul: "really enjoyed our evening together and look forward to breakfast □, Raoul" Gabi smiled; yes it had been a really great evening, and it had been such fun to dance again. The second one was from a certain Irishman. "Was thinking about you all day. What am I doing with my life? And how on earth could I let you go to Hollywood of all places on your own...those sharks will eat you alive, no doubt! Joking aside; please be careful, don't believe everything they say and promise and do NOT allow them to get away with major changes to your beautiful novel! Ach...I know you don't need me to worry about you...just look after yourself. You will always be in my heart...xxx Paddy"

Oh dear, Paddy seemed to be getting soft. Gabi got up and went to the shower without answering any text. She would see Raoul shortly, and Paddy...it would do him good to have to wait a bit.

She came to really enjoy the work with Raoul; he was knowledgeable and accepted her limits – both in work and outside of it. She had no intention to allow the harmless flirt and friendly banter with Raoul to grow into anything more serious. In her heart there was currently still no free room; and she certainly did not want to endanger their good working relationship or complicate her own life with a long-distance romantic relationship. Life was good as it was right now. The days flew by, her last evening in Hollywood was upon her. The script was done, and Raoul would see the project through from there on. Everyone seemed to like what they had achieved, including the director and the main actors. She met Raoul in the hotel bar for a farewell drink.

"Good evening beautiful lady." He kissed her on the cheek and then grabbed her hand, while sitting down next to her at the bar. "I will really miss you, Gabi...are you sure, you can't stay a bit longer?"

"Raoul, I don't belong here. My home is in England, my family and my life are there. It was great to experience Hollywood, and I am so grateful for the chance to see my novel come to life...and I really enjoyed the time we spent together...however it was always just going to be a visit."

"You could make California your home and bring your loved ones over...you will be earning a lot of money with this movie!"

Gabi smiled and pressed his hand. "It is...complicated, Raoul."

He looked at her and simply nodded. "Ok then let us have a night to remember! Two Margaritas please!"

They enjoyed their cocktails, spent some time on the dance floor and finally ended up outside of Gabi's room. "I really like you, Gabi!" Raoul leant in for a kiss.

Gabi's head was very light. A part of her really wanted to allow herself this bit of fun, another part brought up the image of a certain Irishman. While she was still thinking, Raoul's lips found hers, and with his free hand he pushed the door to her suite open.

He could feel her resistance growing feeble. His lips wandered down her neck, while he closed the door. "Your skin is amazing! So soft…"

"Oh Raoul, you should…."

"…leave?"

"No too late for that…" She kicked her shoes off and pulled him with her to the big bed. They hastily undressed each other and then gave in to desire and lust until they were both satiated and exhausted. Gabi lay in Raoul's arms and smiled at him. "You had this planned!"

Raoul grinned. "From the moment I saw you, yes. You are such an exciting woman in so many ways…and I must say, you really are very hot!!"

Gabi let her fingers play with his hairy chest and smiled at herself. "I feel like a cougar!"

"Ridiculous….I am only a few years younger than you…and you are so sexy…" He softly pushed her down in the cushions and kissed her from top to bottom and back up to her middle. His lips moved from her navel to the inside of her thighs until she groaned; then he took her again.

**30.**

When she took her seat in the plane home to England, Gabi looked and felt like the cat that had the cream. It had been amazing to give in to Raoul; she felt like a woman again...since Paddy had left out of the blue, she had banished all thoughts about men and sex. Raoul had definitely cured her and brought her back to her passionate self. She would most probably not see him again, definitely not for a long time; that did not seem to be important. It had been fun, hot adult fun and passion, liberating and utterly satisfying. After all she was not answerable to anyone, she was a single woman...even though her heart still yearned for that crazy unreliable Irishman.

She settled herself in for the long flight home. Due to not having had much sleep the previous night, she soon snoozed off. She found herself back home in Cornwall...Jago and Demelza were sitting at her table, holding hands. Martha was serving one of her fabulous rosemary lamb roasts. She could feel a man's hand touching her arm tenderly. She turned round to look at him, however she could not see his face...instead she heard her name softly spoken...and opened her eyes. The steward smiled at her.

"Sorry to disturb you, Ma'am. I just wondered, if you would like to have anything to eat and drink?"

She stifled a little yawn and nodded. "Yes that would be very nice, thank you."

He nodded and told her which choices she had. She picked her selection and asked for a strong coffee while waiting. When he had left again, she checked the time and was astonished to realise that she must have been asleep for at least 5 hours. She smiled at herself...not a spring chicken anymore; passionate nights took their toll. Worth it though...she got her current read out and was enjoying the novel with her coffee. Then dinner, a drink or two with a movie, more sleep and when she arrived in London, she was actually feeling quite fresh. She got her car and soon found herself on the way to pick up Demelza. There was a touch of frost on the ground, but the main roads were free and well gritted. When she reached the Poor Clares, she hardly recognised Demelza who had swapped her nun's habit for some casual clothes.

"Lovely to see you again, Gabi. I really am excited to go back home and to learn more about my granddaughter." She hugged Gabi and then took a step back: "How rude of me....do you want a break and a hot drink, before we set off?"

Gabi smiled. "To be fair, a coffee would be nice. I have to say, you look really stunning, Demelza!"

Demelza blushed and took Gabi to the kitchen, where a kettle was quickly boiling and providing a hot drink. "How was your trip to the dream factory? Successful, I have no doubt?"

Gabi smiled, briefly remembering her last night in L.A. "Yes, thank you. I think it will be a great movie. It was an interesting time, I enjoyed the glimpse of Hollywood...however I must admit, that kind of life would not be me for every day of the year. Still I am more than grateful for the chance, the opportunity to work with the highly skilled people there and the experience of the filmset. Being back home now though, that is my real life. Shall we set off then? Have you packed everything you need?"

"Yes I have. My adventure begins now." She smiled at Gabi and quickly pressed her arm with fondness. "Thank you for finding me."

Gabi smiled back. "It all had to happen. We are brought together with the right people at the right moment – at least that is what I believe."

From the car Gabi rang Martha to let her know that they were now on the way.

'Good to hear from you again, Gabi. Emma is already excited to see you both; she even baked a cake...and a very nice one, I have to say. Dinner will be ready, when you arrive."

During the drive the two women realised, that they really had a lot of things in common, even though their paths in life had been very different. Eventually Gabi talked about Paddy and the fact that she still missed him, not in a painful way though. "It is as if he still occupies my heart and soul...I don't even blame him for his disappearing act. I just really remember our good times together and wish that I could hear, smell and feel him again."

If two people are meant to be together, then they will be together again – at a time that God deems right. Sometimes we need to have a break from each other, go our very own path for a while, learn individually, have other experiences and then meet again as a more rounded person ready for and worthy of the other one. I have a feeling that you and Paddy will be re-united for good."

Mhm – there is the old saying: Everything comes to be that waits. Who knows...the main thing is to always remember that you must not rely on someone else for your happiness, instead rather make yourself happy and radiate your positivity out to the universe. Thus you will attract more positive things to your life."

And with that they arrived. As soon as they had parked up, the door opened and Molly came dashing out. Martha and Emma stood in the door, cardigans pulled around their waists.

Good to be home! Hello you crazy dog!!" Gabi ruffled the dog's fur and then let her run and sniff at Demelza who stroked her. Emma came out. She first hugged Gabi and then stood in front of her newly found grandmother unsure of what to do. Demelza just pulled her close and breathed in the lovely smell of her hair. They quickly got all the luggage in and gathered in front of the fire for a cuppa before dinner.

"So, here we all are – a house full of women!" Molly barked once and then stretched out in front of the fireplace.

"So...what do I call you?" Emma looked at Demelza, admiring her stunning looks in normal clothes.

"Whatever you like, my Darling. I guess it is all a bit unusual and new for everyone..."

"I would love to welcome you as my nan in my life."

Demelza smiled at her with tears in her eyes. "I'ld like that very much."

Gabi smiled at Demelza. "Tomorrow I think we should have a stroll to the harbour and see what and who you still recognise."

Demelza looked at her with knowing eyes. "Yes, I think it is a good idea to have a walk around. And maybe then have a hot drink in the pub before going home."

"Exactly my thought."

They enjoyed dinner, some chitchat and a drink afterwards and then a good sleep after all the excitement of the day. In the morning Gabi was greeted by a message from the past.

>How was LA? I cant wait to see your movie on the big screen. Surely you have broken a few Californian hearts ☐ Thinking of you, Paddy xx<

A pang of guilt filled her heart for a moment, allowing the memory of Raoul to enter her mind. Then she smiled and put that back in the memory drawer, where it belonged. So....Paddy was still thinking of her. That filled her heart with warmth and joy. No matter what happens, there is this one love, this one person that will stay with you for the rest of your life...most likely because that particular person really is your soulmate. And the two souls will continue to yearn for each other until they are eventually reunited sometime, somewhere. Oh Paddy...and then Gabi could not help thinking about Demelza and Jago. They had been forcefully separated when they were young and in love; their lives had been very different, however they both had continued to carry the image of the other one in their hearts through the decades. And now they would meet again...what would they be feeling, thinking and expecting? Would they still see each other through the eyes of the teenagers Smiling Gabi got up and got herself sorted for the new day and all that was waiting ahead. Before going downstairs, she took her mobile and decided to send Paddy a quick reply.

>LA was amazing and a great experience in many ways. I do think that they will make a wonderful movie...and I am happy to say that they are really following my novel

Hope you are keeping well...not long until Christmas now. Demelza is with us at the moment, and we are just about to meet Jago. Life is good. ▢<

Only an hour later she was walking with Demelza and Emma down to the harbour. They strolled along the pebbly beach for a bit, wrapped up well against the winter winds. Demelza took in all the scenery that brought back childhood memories. She laughed with tears in her eyes.

"I had almost forgotten just how beautiful this bay is, how amazingly crisp the air feels...and those varying shades of blue and turquoise...!" She hugged Emma. "You as a painter must be especially inspired by all this."

"Oh I am. I have always loved to find a quiet rock and just paint the sea, the bay, the people...it sure is a great place to call home." Emma gave her grandmother a kiss on the cheek and ran ahead to the opening of the caves where they had eventually found the skeletons of Emblyn, her baby and her lover.

Gabi looked at Demelza. "Those caves connect to the ones under our house...where we eventually found your sister." Demelza closed her eyes in silent prayer. She had often thought of her beautiful young sister...so much in love and so convinced that her tall and handsome stranger would do right by her and the baby...do men actually understand the power they hold over a woman's life? Even today, when women are so much better educated, stronger and far more independent, yes even today women allow themselves to be weakened by love and promises. She made the sign of the cross, took a few deep breaths and then turned to Gabi: "Thank you for putting her spirit to rest. And thank you for finding me and allowing me to connect with my gorgeous granddaughter and to reconnect with...my past."

Gabi just nodded. She could not have acted in any other way. And now the next piece of the puzzle would be put into place. The women all turned back towards the harbour pub. They ordered hot toddies to warm themselves up and sat down at a small table in one of the bay windows. Emma and Gabi looked at each other. No sign of Jago yet. While they were warming up nicely and enjoying the view, Jago entered, ordered his usual and sat down two tables away from them. He did not see them, well he really would not have expected them. Emma spotted him and was about to get up; Gabi pressed her back into her chair with a little smile.

"Demelza, look at the gentleman to the right, alone at the table, wearing a thick blue jumper." Demelza turned her head. Her right hand went up to rest over her heart. "Kerensa Jago" she whispered and slowly got up. She walked across to the table where her childhood sweetheart was sitting. When he could feel her presence, he looked up. He just stared at her, his eyes filling with tears.

"Demelza..." He got up and took her hands in his. Then he pulled her close and just held her in his embrace for several minutes.

"Emma, this is without a doubt the most romantic scene I have ever witnessed!" Gabi whispered to Emma in a tearful voice. Emma just nodded. "It is simply beautiful. Through all those years of separation their love for each other has stayed with them and is practically palpable, visible now. I must paint that..."

31

Having left Demelza with Jago to catch up in privacy, Gabi and Emma walked home. "It will be a very special Christmas this year!" Emma linked her arm with Gabi.

"Yes I believe you are right! Would you like to also ask your mum to join us at a time convenient for her during the festive period?"

"Yes, well, I thought about it. I am not sure though...you know, with him being there...I would like to see her actually. I thought that if she feels that she cannot leave him or does not feel free to do so, then I could maybe at least meet her for a stroll on one of the days."

"Good idea. Propose your thoughts to her, tell her that your grandmother is here, too. Make sure that she knows that she is welcome anytime, but that you understand her difficult situation and do not want to put any additional pressure on her."

"Yes, I will give her a ring and have a brief chat. When is your family from Germany arriving again?? And Nick will be here in 10 days..."

Gabi looked at the young woman, whose face had now taken on a beautiful rosy colour. Young love was indeed something special; and it was good that the two young people she loved the most in this world had actually fallen for each other. "You two will have a very special Christmas, that is for sure!" she said with a big smile.

The next few weeks went by in a flash. So much happened, so much needed to be organised. The big Christmas tree, all kinds of decorations, presents were wrapped, foodie treats prepared, guest rooms aired – the house was a hive of activity. Demelza announced that she had let the Mother Superior know that she would not return to the convent. She and Jago had rekindled their relationship and wanted to make the most of their remaining years together. Gabi had a few more appointments regarding her work and then finally got into the Christmas mood herself, when her family arrived from Germany and her son from university. It was two days before Christmas Eve, the table in the kitchen had been extended to its maximum capacity; the house breathed joy and happiness, laughter and love. Everyone was in high spirits. Conversations were held in German and English, with hands and a lot of laughter. Gabi smiled at her nephews who made good attempts at translating for their dad who only spoke some English. Emma and Nick took Molly for a walk; Demelza was now staying with Jago, but both were going to join for the Christmas celebrations. Gabi sat with her mum in front of the lit fireplace, her sister and family had gone for a stroll to the harbour and Martha was busy in the kitchen.

"You have done really well for yourself. I am proud of you." Gabi's mum put her hand on her daughter's. "And while building up your business and writing all your books, you have also managed to raise a wonderful young man. He will no doubt be a successful lawyer...and he now has this beautiful and charming girl-friend. She really seems very nice."

"Emma is perfect for Nick; she has had a hard time, however she has not allowed herself to be beaten by it all. She took stock and has taken charge of her life. She is an amazing painter, really talented. It might well be that she will follow Nick up to Manchester, and then there will just be Martha, Molly and me here."

Her mum looked at her and detected the little trace of sadness in her daughters' eyes. "Your dad would be so proud of you, too. You have mastered many storms yourself...and you have never given up. If that Irishman knows what is good for him, he will be back...mark my words."

Gabi chuckled. "We will see, Mum. I have my writing....and next year my movie will be in the cinemas. I really can't complain. Life is good. Just a shame that Dad couldn't live to see all this."

"He sees it, don't you worry. He and your granny are both up there smiling down on you, on all of us." The two women hugged, Gabi put some more wood on the fire and went to get her mum another mug of coffee. When she returned, she looked at her mum. In her own mind and heart her mum was still the mum who had raised her; realistically though she now was an older woman, in her eighties, with aches and pains; and her main pain was that she had had to let her husband go quite a few years ago now. The evil cancer had destroyed the body of the man she had loved and shared all her adult life with; the father of her daughters who at any point would have given his life for his family. Sometimes both Gabi and her sister got the impression that their mother was readying herself to join her late husband. Gabi stroked her mum's face. "I miss our face to face conversations. I know we speak on the phone most days, but nothing beats being able to look at each other, hug and getting comfort in each other's presence."

"You big softie!" Her mother smiled at her. "Tell me more about Hollywood! It must have been exciting to actually be at the place where dreams are made into movies. And to work with those people..." Gabi nodded and told her mum about the movie settings, the glamour party and how everyone had really been unexpectedly nice to her...some of course extremely nice...She kept that bit to herself. Soon enough all the others came back, and the house was filled with youthful energy again, laughter and pre-Christmas glow. Gabi and her sister went out to the back of the house to fill the big bird table with seeds and peanuts, put more suet filled coconut halves up and have a little chat in the crisp winter air just between the two of them.

"I do admire you, little sis." Gabi smiled at her younger sister. "You have managed to make your marriage last, keep your job down and raise my nephews to be such great and independent lads who already seem to know what they want to do with themselves when they leave school. And you are still very pretty."

Frederike blushed. "To me that is just normal routine. Whereas I have always and will always admire you – you have shown extraordinary bravery in going your way again and again. You are now a successful writer and speaker – you are even having a Hollywood movie made based on one of your novels. Nick – well what can I say; he is such a credit to you, and you alone! I have always had Gerd's support; but you have really brought Nick up on your own; and now he is soon going to be a solicitor. Amazing. And you have taken Emma on, solved the ghost story and reunited Demelza and Jago. You have the biggest heart I have come across...and I really love and admire you!"

"Flannel talk – as Paddy would have said!!" Gabi hugged her sister and walked on with her, arm in arm, over the crisp field.

"Have you heard from him again?" Frederike looked at her sister. "Mhm, a text now and then. Neither of us has actually picked up the phone to speak."

"I think you both are still in love – I reckon the Irishman will be back. The question is: will you have him back?"

Gabi took a deep breath. Her little Hollywood romance popped up in her mind and caused her to smile.

"Have you met someone else?" Frederike looked at her and stopped walking.

"Well...yes and no. I have had a fling in Hollywood – it just felt right...however he was not Paddy. And thus, in answer to your question: yes I still love that mad Irishman and will have him back...IF he finds his way back without my encouragement. It has to be by his own desire to do so. Realistically though I think I should let him go."

"Quite right!! And now...that fling...an actor? I need to know more!!" Frederike pulled her sister's arm.

Gabi just pointed at her nose. "What happens in Hollywood, stays in Hollywood!"

"As if ever! Come on, spill!!" Gabi smiled and then told her sister in a few sentences about Raoul and their brief encounter.

"Wow – so...are you contemplating following his invitation to move to Hollywood...to be with him and give it a chance?"

Gabi firmly shook her head. "No – it is not my world. This here is. And I really am happy here. I have so much to be utterly grateful for; and I enjoy the pace of life in this part of the world. I have found my rhythm, and it suits me."

"Then that is all that matters, Gabi."

The sisters went back to the house. That night Gabi found herself reflecting on her life, the changes The Secret had brought and the realisation that she needed to set Paddy free properly by sending him the engagement ring back. As much as she loved him and knew that he truly cared for her, she understood that Paddy was a true wandering spirit and could not, at least not yet, settle happily in one place. She got her writing paper out and started a letter to him, reflecting on their time together, the countless beautiful moments, the laughter and tenderness shared, the mutual understanding and support. Ending the note with " ... and so it is with deep gratitude in my heart that I have been allowed to share your life for a while and to make lasting, beautiful memories with you, that I can now set you free. It was one of the happiest moments in my life, when you asked me to marry you; however understand you that well that I know you must not be tied down, you need to roam freely. And after all a bird with clipped wings is not really a bird anymore. So my Darling Paddy I am returning the engagement ring to you and wish you only the best for the years ahead. We both believe in the Law of Attraction and have experienced enough proof to know that The Secret works. Some people come into your life to help you through some darker times and leave when their work is done; that is how I like to see your time in my life. Absolutely no hard feelings, only love and gratitude. Yours Gabi" She folded the paper and put it and the ring in a padded envelop with the family address in Cork. She sighed, smiled and went to bed.

32

It was a truly magical Christmas for everyone. Martha loved being part of this extended family and being able to show off her culinary skills, supported by all the other women in the house when needed. Christmas Eve they enjoyed a traditional German potato salad accompanied with different types of sausages and cold meat, champagne and homemade cookies for afters. The fire was roaring, they were singing traditional carols, then listening to music and playing games. Nick and Emma were cuddled close together, the boys sat on the floor with the dog next to them; Demelza and Jago were visibly happy and relaxed, at ease with each other and the world that had finally granted them the peace and love they had longed for so long. Gabi loved having all her family under one roof; it was good to have her mum here, her sister and family, her son in his new loved-up state. She sat in the back and squeezed Martha's hand. "Thank you Martha for making all this possible; I could not have got it all sorted in time without you. I really am glad we have found each other!"

Martha actually blushed. "It is lovely to have a house filled with all this love and laughter at this special time of the year. And what a fine couple Nick and Emma make!"

Gabi smiled. "Yes indeed. I could not have wished for a finer young woman for my son. We really are blessed. I know we have all had our share of heartache and pain in the past, however there is so much to be grateful for. And the celebrations have only just begun."

After everyone had retired to bed, Gabi started reflecting on when her life had changed for the better. She could pinpoint the moment when one of her friends had told her about "The Secret" – the formula for making the Law of Attraction work for you; learning to control your thoughts and slowly but surely switching your whole mindset from negative, anxious and fearful to positive, inspired and achieving. As a single mum she had been struggling to make ends meet, even though she worked tirelessly and stretched herself all the time. She loved her son and wanted to give him all she could, which often did not quite compare with what his friends had. However Nick never complained, but understood. The bond between mother and son was extremely strong; he was her greatest gift in life. And when she learned about the LOA and came to understand that you are the master of your life, the director of the movie called your life, that your thoughts control what you attract through the mindset you create with them, she made sure to teach him as well. And he learned and became a very confident and loving young man – a young man who was understanding and caring in a way that enabled him to attach a vulnerable young woman like Emma to himself and give her all the tenderness she needed to thrive. And she herself? Well, she had gone on to grow the courage to publish her first books, take time out for herself and her personal development every day, went from strength to strength, to better jobs and finally got the opportunity to set herself free from the rat race and buy this house and live her dream of just writing and teaching other people to follow her example. And of course she had attracted the almost ideal male into her life...

Of course the Law of Attraction does not mean you can sit back and just wait for things to come to you; while you become more and more aware of the way you think and what you focus on, you then shift from negative, from worrying and procrastinating to taking control of your life and pushing for becoming what you want to be and getting to a place where you want to be. It is all a matter of your attitude. Amazing things happen when you change your outlook on the world; you do see a somehow brand new world in brighter colours, you attract people that are like minded and will support you on your way directly or indirectly. You decide what you want to achieve and you take responsibility for getting there. Once you declare yourself open for the influx of opportunities and once you start seeing changes as chances and not threats, you step out confidently into this world and claim your rightful place. You deserve to be happy and fulfilled – so go for it.

She knew that The Secret and the LOA influenced her life, the way she thought and acted, and also her writing. She was particularly pleased to see that it had helped her to have the peaceful strength to let go of the man she really loved, most likely for the benefit of both of them. It was not right to try and tie someone down who could just not fully be himself in a settled down relationship; it caused pain to both sides...after all it is not a satisfying feeling to think that the person next to you is only still with you, because he is afraid to leave, but his heart is not in it all. The fact that he had tried his best made her happy and feel special. And her life was so full with good people and rewarding work, that she did not need to feel upset. Sometimes people come into your life to help you for a while and then move on again...like Mary Poppins. She smiled to herself and kept that smile and deep gratitude all over Christmas and New Year. The house was so full of laughter and love, joy and happiness, good food and great conversations – no one could complain at all about anything being amiss.

And no one did. Martha was in her element with loads of people to feed and water, the laughter of children in the house and all the special smells of the season -

cinnamon, spiced apples and oranges, incense cones, scented candles, the turkey...and with so many women in the house, the cleaning up was quickly sorted every time. Demelza and Jago joined the enlarged household for most of the dinners; however they also enjoyed going for walks on their own, catching up on the lost years and being at ease in each other's company. Demelza loved the old rugged man just as dearly as she had the young and handsome lad; Jago was in awe of the beautiful lady God had given back to him after all these years...and he truly enjoyed being the envy of many a man in the town. Gabi's mum loved the area, the house and most of all having all her loved ones around in such harmony and well-being. Frederike and her family simply enjoyed the beauty of the scenery, the great conversations and the break from daily routine, the relaxed mode and the amazing food provided by Martha. They had brought home made Christmas cookies from Germany to add to the menu, spiced winter tea and special delicacies to give Gabi that warm feeling of childhood memories. Nick and Emma were inseparable. They entertained Nick's young cousins, took the dog for walks and simply reminded everyone of what it was like to be young and in love, with everything to live for ahead of you, millions of plans in your head and the utter conviction that you will create the life of your dreams together. And thanks to early exposure to the teachings of the Secret and the Law of Attraction Nick owned the tools to be confident and successful, and his calm and knowledgeable way of being had also helped and influenced Emma for the better. They were a lovely couple now, and Gabi had no doubt that they would continue to be a stable and positive influence in each other's life for the future. Some couples just ooze that quiet confidence and trust in each other; they do not need to talk about it, post about their love in social media, they just live it and enjoy life together. Gabi smiled to herself – she was definitely much better in passing on her knowledge and thus helping others live strong and healthy relationships than she was following her advice herself. Then again, is it maybe experience of how things should not be that enables the good teacher to help others walk the better path? We live and learn – if we allow ourselves to be open to what the universe is trying to teach us. And when we have understood and taken the learning from our experiences, it surely is a good thing to then pass our findings on to others and enable them to avoid certain pitfalls by becoming aware ahead of time. Apart from having conversations with the people you care about and those who seek your advice, an ideal way to pass on what the universe had taught you was in Gabi's case incorporating her understanding in her novels. People have stories to tell, the universe shows you stories – you just need to be open minded and willing to listen and learn.

33

The year was coming to an end. New Year's Eve meant it was time to let go of the old and embrace the new, the new opportunities, new chances ahead. The women had prepared a buffet spread in the big kitchen; everyone could just choose what they fancied all through the evening. January 2nd would be when everyone was going to go back to the demands of their normal everyday life. Gabi's family would fly back to Germany. The house would slowly empty.

"Mum, we would like to talk about something to you." Nick and Emma took Gabi aside.

"I guess, you want to tell me that you are both going up to Manchester the day after tomorrow?"

Emma smiled. "I told you that your mum already knows anyhow."

"Well, watching you two over the holidays has made it obvious that you want to be together. And why not. Nick has enough space in Manchester for both of you. Just promise me that you will not distract each other from the chosen career but instead support each other on the way."

"Of course, mum. And we will make it all a success. Plus we will still be in touch with you regularly." Nick gave his mum a hug.

"I will miss you two, of course. Still letting go is part of life...and for you two the next phase has started. You might want to tell your mum and gran, too, Emma."

"Yes. We will tell Demelza tonight and try and see mum tomorrow."

Gabi poured three glasses of Prosecco. "Here is to new beginnings then!"

Just as they happily cheered each other, Demelza actually came to talk to them – as if she was pulled by an invisible force. "It is not midnight yet...what are you three celebrating?"

"We were toasting to new beginnings." Nick smiled and poured another glass for Demelza. He nodded to Emma.

"We have just told Gabi that I will be accompanying Nick to Manchester when he goes back in two days' time. I intend to study Art while Nick finishes his Law degree. We..."

Demelza smiled. "You want to be together and not waste time...I understand. Good on you two! Gabi and I will have to content with holiday visits then." Demelza hugged her grand-daughter and then Nick. "Make the most of your time – the years fly by so quickly. I look forward to coming up to Manchester for your first exhibition!" Emma blushed and squeezed Nick's hand. "I can only thank you all...what an outstanding year this has turned out to be – it certainly brought about many changes for me that I am truly grateful for. And I have learned so much...about myself and the world...and of course my family – well actually what family really means."

"Time to get ready for the big countdown!" Martha interrupted them preparing champagne flutes and a big plate with donuts and a huge German New Year's Brezel made of yeast dough. Jago had opened the veranda door to give them direct view to the sea and the harbour which was beautifully lit up. In the background the TV was on, so that they could follow the official countdown to the new year – another moment for people cheering and putting all their hopes and wishes, dreams and ambitions into three words and countless hugs and kisses: "Happy New Year"!

Of course they all stayed up until the early hours of the morning, some longer, some went to bed earlier. Gabi's mum was the first to say her good nights – this was way past her usual bedtime. The last ones to sit around the fire were Gabi and her son. Emma had given in to her tiredness and gone to bed. Gabi looked at her grown-up son. "You look the happiest I have ever seen you." She gave him a hug.

"I am, Mum. My studies are going well, and being with Emma is such bliss. She is so easy to be with...so different to other girls."

"She is a gem. And I am glad for her sake that she can be with you. She had a lot to deal with in her past after all."

"Yes, she is doing very well though. She is tough and positive – like you in a way."

Gabi smiled. "Time to go to bed for me, too."

"Have you heard from him?" Nick asked getting up. "You know that he will be back. He adores you, Mum!"

"I heard from him every now and again. I finally sent him the engagement ring back. I want him to know that he is free – and I hold no grudges at all. I am grateful for the time with Paddy and the memories we have made. Maybe he will come back one day when he has finally conquered all his demons. And until then I will remain happy on my own."

"You do seem to be ok with it all. I am glad that you have this strength inside of you to always carry on. It is good to know that I do not need to worry about your happiness."

"Oh Darling, you don't! I am fine; of course I think about him, and there are times when I miss him. All in all however I am indeed happy with my life and all that I have achieved and all the wonderful people that are in it. Let us see what this new year will hold for us."

"You certainly are a strong woman and a great role model, mum. I am proud to be your son." Nick kissed his mother on the cheek and left to go upstairs.

Gabi smiled and watched the last ambers in the fireplace. While she loved her family, loved entertaining and having friends round, she had also always relished those moments of calm after everyone had retreated and she could be alone with herself and her thoughts or just enjoy a few minutes of meditation. It was good to go through the events of the day, the last few days and now the whole last year. The ups and downs, the surprises, the memories that were made, the people that had come into her life, those that had left or that she had left behind. There certainly was a constant flux, life had never been boring for her – challenging sometimes and hard a lot of times, however she had always found a way to get up and go on. Really once she had understood the Law of Attraction and learned to control her thoughts, it had become easy to manage life. Manage your attitude, your thoughts, and not the issues life throws at you. Manage how you filter and process all that your mind picks up on in a day, and you have found the magic switch. Now she felt that it was her turn to empower others, particularly other women to step out of the shadows and confidently into the light, to stand up and speak up for themselves and to become the best version of themselves in order to achieve their dreams. With a "can do" attitude all becomes possible, achievable.

Gabi thought about Emma. When she had met her, the poor girl had given up on herself, on life and humankind. Now she had the confidence of a young warrior, stood and walked proudly and had learned that not only was she worth of other people's love, she also had a lot of love to give. And she had allowed herself to develop her artistic talent. She would go all the way. Gabi decided to use Emma's story in her next empowerment workshop. It was an inspiring story and needed to be shared. There were still so many women out there who had lost hope, faith, confidence and their love for life. They just needed to be heard and supported to open themselves up to the gift the universe held ready for them.

34

They had said their good-byes to Gabi's family. Her brother-in-law drove the hire car back to London with a stop somewhere in Cornwall or Devon that might take their fancy. It had been great to have them all round and spend time with them, particularly at this special time of the year. Gabi loved her family, and she cherished all her childhood memories; and there were still times when she really wanted to talk to her dad again who had passed on now almost 6 years ago. Love and closeness never die – you just find a different way of communication with the departed loved ones.

Emma and Nick would be leaving the following day. They had just taken Molly for a walk, as soon as Klaus had driven off. They were walking through the bracken towards the now sealed again entry to the caverns where the skeletons had been found. "Strange, isn't it, how without Emblyn's tragedy we all might never have grown together as we did...I mean, my nan Demelza is back where she belongs and with the man she wants to be with; we all worked out the secret of the skeletons together, which...helped me get over my home experiences, grow in so many ways...and even helped bring us together." Emma stopped and wrapped her arms around Nick. He looked at her.

"Em, you are tougher than you give yourself credit for. You have had to face things that still make me angry and upset in equal measures. However you never gave up on love and trust; first you put all your trust in mum – and of course Paddy and Martha; and then you let me in to your life. You are all that I have dreamed about and more – beautiful, clever, talented, strong and warm. I promise to always be there for you and to always be honest and supportive. I do think it was all meant to be...us moving here – which at first I was not at all happy about as a city dweller...mum and Paddy starting this counselling group, you being courageous enough to seek mum out for help...I love you." He pulled her close and kissed her. Molly had sat down a little ahead of them and seemed to watch them.

"I love you, Nick. You may not ever fully understand it, but you are my saviour in many ways. And your mum is simply amazing – I am so grateful to her, because she has given me my life back....no, she has showed me to build my own life." Emma took Nick's hand, and they followed the dog for a nice walk in the winter sun.

Martha had watched the young couple for a little while. She knew that Gabi was a great mother...actually to Nick and Emma both. And she knew that Gabi missed her son...she would now have to miss Emma, too. Empty nest syndrome? While Gabi was a strong woman, she also was someone who felt emotions deeply and acted with passion. Still...good the two women had each other. Martha smiled and made a pot of tea.

The next day they were waving off Nick and Emma. Molly was winging, Martha sighing and Gabi had tears in her eyes. Demelza had come to join the good-bye and looked both happy for her grand-daughter and somewhat sad for having to part from her for a while. When the taxi to the station was out of sight, the three women closed the door and gathered round the big wooden kitchen table for mugs of tea.

"If in doubt, have a cuppa!" Martha boiled the kettle.

"They will be fine – they have their individual talents, each other and their love." Demelza smiled.

"And they have all of us having their back." Gabi took a deep breath. Even though she of course was in favour of letting the young couple go and carve their own way in life by and by, she still always felt a lump inside, when she had to say good-bye to her son. Empty nest syndrome...another form of grief that you just need to accept and learn to live with. What you know and what you feel are not always the same thing; she would be fine again in a day or two – once she was back into her own balanced routine of work and leisure. As an added plus there was now Demelza to add to her circle of local friends.

The three women all had a quiet moment while sipping their tea. Demelza broke the silence first. "How about me cooking a nice dinner tonight, and the two of you coming round and joining the old skipper and me?"

Martha and Gabi looked at each other. "Great, that will be lovely."

Martha quite enjoyed having someone else cook the dinner and sort everything that goes with it. Demelza had prepared a traditional Stargazy pie, however without the fish heads sticking out the pie crust. It was delicious and washed down with a local ale. They all enjoyed each other's company and light-hearted conversation. Jago seemed to have taken to his new role as host very smoothly; he actually quite enjoyed looking after the three ladies. Having Demelza back in his life, having her live with him under one roof in his fisherman's cottage was something he could still hardly believe; the dream of his life had come true in the end. And he knew that he had Gabi to thank for.

"Let me say a toast at the beginning of this year, amongst friends. A big thank you to Gabi here who reached out to an old man for help with solving a long buried secret. You encouraged me to make some changes to my sad routine...and most of all you are directly responsible for bringing the love of my life back to me. Never will I be able to thank you enough...to Gabi, a good gal who has made an old man very happy!!"

Gabi blushed, Demelza smiled and Martha just added: "Well said...to Gabi!!"

Gabi recovered from her moment of embarrassment and raised the glass again: "Let us toast all the people and things we can be utterly grateful for. While it is good to focus on your goals and plans for the future, every now and again it is equally important to stop and reflect on all that we have achieved already. All in all it was a good year, this one we just finished...just for myself, I won new friends, gained a daughter in Emma, won a Hollywood contract, have reached many people with my publications and speaking events and hopefully managed to help them a bit, enjoyed a fabulous year in this beautiful place and had some amazing times with my crazy Irishman; we all together solved the Secret around the skeletons in the cave and managed to put their souls to rest. Not bad for one year. Cheers to us all!!"

An hour later Martha and Gabi said their farewells and walked home through the frosty winter air. "Well my dear, let us see what this year will bring!"

"Indeed Martha. First of all though – a good night's sleep for both of us".

35

Gabi returned from a nice walk with Millie, when Martha greeted her somewhat distressed. "Gabi, I might have to leave you for a few weeks. I just had a phone call from my cousin Dorothy."

Gabi dried the dog's paws, washed her hands and put the kettle on. "Let me make us a cuppa, then you can tell me everything in peace."

With the steaming tea in front of them and the dog resting by their feet, Martha started summing up the call from her cousin. "Dorothy and I used to be really close as children and teenagers. Then she got a job in the city, married, had no children...anyhow she is a widow now. She is 65 and had a bad fall; she broke her right leg. They say that they will let her go back home, if she can find a carer for the next 3 weeks or so. I would like to go and look after her, Gabi."

"Of course, Martha. You must. I can see that it is important to you – and for the next two months I have no travels planned at all. So take all the time you need and do not worry...I can look after Millie and myself for a while; I will miss your company of course; however your cousin clearly has greater needs than me. Can I help with anything?"

"No Gabi, I will be alright. Maybe a lift to the station, once I have packed and got myself organised."

"Of course Martha. I hope that you two will have a good time down memory lane as well as Dorothy recovering quickly. Bones don't heal as fast when you are older. She will be in the best hands, when you are there." Gabi gave Martha a big hug. "And seriously if you need anything, just give me a call."

Martha smiled. "Thanks Gabi...well I better look at train times and start packing."

A few hours later Martha was safely on the train to London. Gabi sat at her desk and stared at her laptop. She still needed to finish the story of the skeletons, however her mind kept wandering. It was a strange world at times. Here she was in this beautiful big house just outside a small Cornish town, all by herself all of a sudden. While she appreciated her own company and deemed it necessary for everyone to maintain time slots for me-time in their everyday schedule, it felt strange to be alone with Millie who seemed to share her feelings, as she had taken position in the doorway between Gabi's office and the big square hall. Millie seemed to be expecting someone. Gabi smiled. "Afraid, it is just you and me for a little while, Moll! Well apart from Demelza popping in with or without Jago. We won't see Emma and Nick until Easter, and Martha needs to nurse her cousin. I think I might have to put some nice background music on and light a few candles."

With Jazz playing on low volume and a few candles lit in her office, she instantly felt more inspired again and managed to write a few paragraphs. Then she closed the laptop and took Millie for a short evening walk. After they both enjoyed a light dinner, Gabi lit the wood burner, poured herself a glass of wine and put on a light hearted movie. Halfway through that, she all of a sudden heard a car stop outside. Millie looked up, but did not give loud. Instead she started wagging her tail.

Gabi got up and walked to the kitchen window from where she could see the driveway very well. She did not recognise the car. Millie had followed her still wagging her tail.

"Millie, I don't know who you think that is. I certainly am not expecting anyone; also I do not know the car. Better safe than sorry." She turned the hall lights on and grabbed hold of Millie's collar. When she was just about to open the door, the door bell went.

Gabi slowly opened. Millie slipped out of her grip and jumped at the person standing there. Gabi's jaw dropped. "You????"

The man on the other side calmed the dog down and sent her back inside. "Yes it is me. I have come home – that is, if you want me back."

Gabi just stared at the man in front of her. "Well to start with, come on in out of the cold, Paddy."

Paddy followed the invite and looked around. "It seems strangely quiet in here. Are you on your own?"

"Yes, home alone with Millie...first night though." Gabi went into the kitchen and put the kettle on. "I guess you could do with a cuppa?"

Paddy nodded, stroked the dog, hung his jacket up in the hall and just looked at her. "You look very well, Gabi!"

"Thanks. You don't look too shabby yourself. Have you driven far?"

Paddy took a deep breath. "Well I woke up in Cork this morning, asked myself what the hell I was doing there, packed and just kept driving. And here I am now."

Gabi shook her head at him. "Very dramatic, Paddy. Have you had something to eat?"

"Not hungry. Cup of tea will suffice."

Gabi put a mug of steaming tea in front of him. "Well then, come to the living room, lets sit in front of the fire...and then explain yourself."

Gabi led the way, put some more wood on the fire and sat down. She signalled for Paddy to sit opposite her. That way she hoped to retain her self-control longer. After all, he really could not expect to appear out of nowhere after all this time and simply pick up the relationship where he had left it months ago.

Paddy seemed to understand and sat down with his tea. "Gabi, I won't even try to apologise or come up with some feeble excuses. The truth is: I panicked all of a sudden. I had this dark cloud come over my head...I felt that it was all too much for me."

Gabi took a sip of her wine and just looked at him. Her instinct was to just take him in her arms, kiss and make love. However that would not be the right approach right now. This time, if there was going to be another time for them, it needed to be a real commitment. No more running away for no obvious reason. She chose to remain silent and wait.

Paddy seemed lost in thoughts. "The moment of realising that I was really heading in the wrong direction was when I received your engagement ring back. That stung. And the little note you sent with it actually made me cry."

Gabi sighed. She got up to put a few more logs on the fire. Also it gave her a good excuse to turn her back on him for a moment, so that she could gather her thoughts. She remembered very well what she had written – she had set him free. Clearly though he did not really want to be free anymore. The prodigal son had returned. Subconsciously she must have done exactly the right thing. Or was it maybe not right – would he disappear into the night again one of those days?? She sighed again. And before she could turn around, she could feel him. He had got up and was standing right behind her. She could even feel his breath against her neck. Good God – would she be able to trust herself now, as she could already feel desire growing rapidly inside of her.

"Gabi, I really love you!" From behind he put his arms around her. Gabi closed her eyes and just enjoyed the feeling of being held, this familiar warmth of the man she still loved. She took a few deep breaths trying to hold this moment for as long as possible. Then she slowly turned round.

"Enough to actually stay? Enough to work with me through the not so exciting days? Enough to have my back, when things go wrong? Enough to actually live a relationship with all the ups and downs?" She looked right into his eyes, where she could see honesty and warmth, tenderness and love and some pain.

"It pains me that you have to ask, mo stor!!"

"Experience, my dear Paddy, experience." She looked at him, wanted to just kiss him and forget the rest; however she knew that she really needed to stand her ground here. "What you must understand is that I do not need you in my life; I can look after myself very well. If I choose to live with you again, then I would do so, because I want you with me and I want to share my life with you."

"I know."

"And I will only consider that option, if you are actually now able to make promises that you will keep."

Paddy sighed deeply. Then he smiled. He let go of her, put his right hand in his pocket and went down on one knee. "Please accept my ring again; the ring to bind us together. I love you. I have loved you from the day we met and never stopped loving you. My demons chased me off a few times – that is not an excuse, just an explanation. You are all that I now want in my life. Please Gabi, forgive me and take me back...and let's get married as soon as possible!" He held the engagement ring up to her.

Gabi felt a big lump in her throat. She had never stopped loving him either. Tears were forming in her eyes. She extended her left hand to him ready to accept the ring on her finger. She nodded. "Yes Paddy, lets do it. Lets stop wasting time, lets be happy together again!"

They just held each other for a while, then allowed passion to take control in front of the last ambers in the wood burner. Giggling they then made their way upstairs and fell asleep to the wind picking up over the sea.

THE END

Printed in Great Britain
by Amazon

32916429R00079